Hello!

Watch out world - Mouse is back!

When I wrote my first book, *Dizzy*, a few years back, I got so many emails and letters asking for a sequel I couldn't quite believe it. *Lucky Star* is not a sequel exactly - you don't have to have read *Dizzy* to read this book - but it picks up on the story of one of the original characters, Mouse, now that he's fourteen. Mouse didn't get a happy ending in *Dizzy*, but in *Lucky Star* . . . well, you'll have to see!

Mouse is my all-time favourite character from any of the books, so I hope you like him too! He doesn't go looking for trouble, but trouble has a way of finding him all the same. When he falls for a cool, cute, confident girl called Cat, Mouse quickly finds himself not just in trouble, but in danger too. Can he trust his new friend, or is she playing a cat and mouse game that can only end in tears?

Lucky Star is a book about friendship, family, fear - and fighting back against injustice to find the magic in life. I think you'll like Mouse's story - it's a rollercoaster ride of drama, love and glad-to-be-alive happiness, set in the shadowy world of a tough inner-city estate. As for luck - you can find it in the most unexpected places!

Keep reading, keep smiling . . . and follow your dreams!

Best Wishes,

Cathy Cassidy x ❄

cathycassidy.com

Books by Cathy Cassidy

DIZZY
DRIFTWOOD
INDIGO BLUE
SCARLETT
SUNDAE GIRL
LUCKY STAR

cathy cassidy

Lucky STAR

PUFFIN

PUFFIN BOOKS

Published by the Penguin Group
Penguin Books Ltd, 80 Strand, London WC2R ORL, England
Penguin Group (USA) Inc., 375 Hudson Street, New York, New York 10014, USA
Penguin Group (Canada), 90 Eglinton Avenue East, Suite 700, Toronto, Ontario, Canada M4P 2Y3
(a division of Pearson Penguin Canada Inc.)
Penguin Ireland, 25 St Stephen's Green, Dublin 2, Ireland (a division of Penguin Books Ltd)
Penguin Group (Australia), 250 Camberwell Road, Camberwell, Victoria 3124, Australia
(a division of Pearson Australia Group Pty Ltd)
Penguin Books India Pvt Ltd, 11 Community Centre, Panchsheel Park, New Delhi – 110 017, India
Penguin Group (NZ), 67 Apollo Drive, Rosedale, North Shore 0632, New Zealand
(a division of Pearson New Zealand Ltd)
Penguin Books (South Africa) (Pty) Ltd, 24 Sturdee Avenue, Rosebank, Johannesburg 2196,
South Africa

Penguin Books Ltd, Registered Offices: 80 Strand, London WC2R ORL, England

puffinbooks.com

First published 2007
This edition produced for The Book People Ltd, Hall Wood Avenue,
Haydock, St Helens WA11 9UL
1

Text copyright © Cathy Cassidy, 2007
Illustrations copyright © Cathy Cassidy, 2007
All rights reserved

The moral right of the author/illustrator has been asserted

Set in Baskerville MT by Palimpsest Book Production Limited,
Grangemouth, Stirlingshire
Made and printed in England by Clays Ltd, St Ives plc

British Library Cataloguing in Publication Data
A CIP catalogue record for this book is available from the British Library

ISBN: 978-1-856-13244-2

www.greenpenguin.co.uk

Penguin Books is committed to a sustainable future
for our business, our readers and our planet.
The book in your hands is made from paper
certified by the Forest Stewardship Council.

Thanks . . .

Thanks, as ever, to Liam, Calum and Caitlin for keeping me sane and putting up with me – also to Mum, Dad, Joan, Andy, Lori and all my fab family for endless love and support. Thanks to my lovely friends, Sheena, Helen, Fiona, Mary-Jane, Zarah and co. for the pep talks, hugs and chocolate, and to my cheerleading fellow writers, Catriona, Meg and Lisa. Also to Paul for the web support, Martyn for doing the adding-up bits, and John for driving the Dizzy-mobile!

Big thanks to Magi for being a fab first reader and offering lots of great insight, and to my editor, Rebecca, for carefully unearthing the story I'd planned to write all along! Thanks too to Amanda, Adele, Francesca, Kirsten, Emily, Ali, Jodie, Katya, Sara, Sarah, Jennie and the whole team at Puffin HQ for being so brilliant, and to best-ever agent Darley and his angels Julia, Lucie, Zoe, Emma and all at the agency.

The last thank you goes to my readers, whose emails, letters and pictures make all the hard work worthwhile. To know that you love the stories as much as I do means everything to me – you're the best!

Flat 114/9
Nightingale House
Eden Estate
Clapham
London SW1

Dear Mr Brown,

I know how mad you are with me right now, and you have every right to be, but I just wanted to say I am really, really sorry. I just didn't think that you'd get so upset about a little bit of paint, but I know better now, obviously.

I don't even know why I did it, except that I like graffiti art and I honestly thought that the wall by the gym could do with brightening up. I guess I was wrong about that. I know now that you prefer that wall to be grey, and that you really didn't like the stars and spirals and rainbows I sprayed all over it.

I admit that writing 'school is cancelled until

further notice' on the wall was not very clever, even though it seemed funny at the time. I'm sorry that some of the kids who saw it decided to use it as an excuse to go right on home. I am also sorry that my spelling wasn't too good, and I know that was what tipped you off that I was to blame. That and the paint on my fingers.

Well, I want you to know I have learnt my lesson. Dave (you remember Dave – my social worker) says I have messed up one time too many, and I need to wise up and make amends or else my school career will be down the pan.

If you like, I will come in to school and paint the whole lot out with grey emulsion paint, so the wall is back to being plain and dull and crumbly. I would have done that already, except for being excluded and everything. Mum says if you see me any time soon with a bucket of paint, you'll most likely call the police, and I guess she has a point.

Anyway, I have turned over a new leaf. I am not going to tag any more walls, unless they are very neglected and really need livening up, and only then if I get permission from the government or something. I am also going to work on my spelling, seriously. If you are wondering how come my spelling is so good in this letter, it's because I did it on Dave's computer and used the spell-check, as I know that stuff like that matters to you.

I know you said that my future at Green Vale Comprehensive is hanging in the balance, but I want you to know that your little talk the other day has really made me think. I didn't say much, but I was taking it all in, I swear. I will be a model pupil from now on. I hope that you will give me one more chance, and I promise never to spray-paint the school again, no matter what.

Yours faithfully,

Mouse (Martin) Kavanagh, Form 9b

> Green Vale Comprehensive,
> 211 Peter Street,
> Clapham
> London SW1

Dear Martin Kavanagh,

I must inform you that the school has already gone to great trouble and expense to paint out the graffiti in question, so your offer to do so will not be necessary. I feel that you still fail to grasp the seriousness of your repeated acts of vandalism. If there are any further incidents of this kind, you are likely to be looking at an anti-social behaviour order, as well as a permanent exclusion.

As things stand, you remain excluded until the October break. I hope to see a marked improvement in your class work, attitude and behaviour once the new term begins.

Yours sincerely,

Mr T. Brown

Head teacher

'He's not a happy man,' Dave says, reading the letter from my head teacher.

'Never has been,' I shrug. 'He worries too much.'

Dave shoots me a dark look. 'At least they're letting you back into school,' he says. 'Your letter showed maturity, Mouse. You apologized, took responsibility for your actions. You realized you were wrong.'

I take a bite of Mars bar, and grin.

'Mouse?' Dave asks, carefully. 'You do know you were wrong, don't you?'

'C'mon, Dave!' I say. 'It was hardly the crime of the century, was it? It was a joke!'

'A joke?' he echoes. 'Mouse, your idea of a joke happens to be most people's idea of mindless vandalism!'

'Mindless? C'mon! That wall looked a whole lot better once I'd tagged it – they should have given me a grant for improving the environment or something.'

5

Dave clenches his teeth, as if he's in pain. He peers at me over the top of his trendy black specs with sorrowful green eyes. 'Mouse, don't you ever learn?' he asks. 'It wasn't easy to persuade Mr Brown to keep the police out of this. You don't need me to tell you what that would have meant . . . you already have a police record.'

'Not a bad one!' I argue. 'Just for tagging a bus stop!'

Dave shakes his head. 'I'm not kidding, Mouse – you can't pull any more stunts like this. Every time things start going well for you, you do something stupid and mess it all up. I'm beginning to think it's a cry for help!'

I just about choke on my Mars bar. 'A cry for help? Are you serious?'

Social workers always think there's a deep, dark reason lurking behind everything you do – some buried trauma that only a psychologist can dig out of you. Bite your nails? You obviously had a deprived childhood. Wear your fringe too long? Must be hiding something. Don't like carrots? Man, you're just about ready for the nut house.

Dave sits back on his trendy black swivel chair, smoothing down his Nirvana T-shirt and crossing his legs in ancient, faded bootleg jeans. He thinks this kind of stuff makes him look cool, friendly, accessible. I think it makes him look like a sad old loser.

'It wasn't a cry for help,' I say. 'It was art!'

'Hmphh,' he says. 'Well. The next time you're feeling arty, buy yourself a sketchbook.'

I laugh out loud. The things I want to say just won't fit between the pages of a sketchbook – they need to be painted six feet tall, by moonlight, with your heart beating fast and your mouth dry with fear.

'Why, Mouse?' Dave asks, giving me this full-on, sad-eyed stare. 'I just don't understand why.'

Dave has this whole range of disappointed, guilt-trip looks he likes to wind me up with, but I refuse to feel bad. I paint on walls because it makes me feel good. That's as much as I'm going to admit – to anyone.

I'm not about to go digging around in the past for a bunch of deep, dark reasons for why I'm not perfect. It's just not up for discussion – all the bad memories are packed away in boxes I'll never need to open again. Start looking at all that and I'd unravel faster than a sweater with a hole in. Seriously – it's just not happening.

Dave shakes his head. 'Out of here, Mouse,' he says. 'Time's up, and we're getting nowhere. At least the school have agreed to take you back after the October break – I suggest you use this time off to reflect. You need to make some changes – and fast.'

7

I stand up, shrug on my zip-up hoodie.

'Thanks for your support and understanding,' I say brightly. 'It means a lot.'

Dave rakes a hand through his hair, exasperated. 'I'm on your side, Mouse,' he says heavily. 'If I get hacked off with you sometimes . . . well, it's because I care.'

That's a laugh. Dave may act like my favourite cheesy uncle, but he's not. He is a social worker – my own personal social worker. It's his job to look out for me, to keep me out of trouble, even though he is clearly not too good at it. He is paid to care.

The way I see it, that just doesn't count.

I scuff my way out of the office, leaving Dave with his head in his hands. Out in the waiting room, a girl looks up from her magazine as I emerge, a pretty, mixed-race girl with honey-coloured skin and slanting eyes. She smiles at me, a long, lazy smile.

'He is not in a good mood,' I tell her, by way of a warning.

'Is he ever?'

She unfolds her long, tawny legs and stands up slowly, like some kind of schoolgirl supermodel. She's in uniform, one of those posh-school jobs, but she looks cool – she's the kind of girl who could probably look cool wearing a potato sack. Her black beret sits rakishly above a mass of golden-brown hair that falls in corkscrew curls to her shoulders.

She looks exotic, somehow, a world apart from the girls at Green Vale Comp, who chew gum with their mouths open and wear their trousers slung low and their heels slung high. This girl is wearing a little green pleated skirt, knee-length grey socks and flat shoes. You wouldn't think that could be cute, but I'm telling you, it can.

'Wish me luck,' she says, throwing me a wink as she disappears into Dave's office.

'Good luck,' I say, even though I haven't believed in luck since my dad left, back when I was seven years old. For her, maybe, I'd reconsider.

I've seen all sorts of kids in the waiting room outside Dave's office over the years, kids who look lost, kids who look lonely, kids who look rough, tough, bad, sad, mad. I've never seen one like her before, though, a girl who looks like she could wrap the world round her little finger, then put it in her pocket for later. I can't help wondering what her story is – how come she's washed up here, in the Clapham Youth Outreach Unit, with dodgy Dave as her official guardian angel?

One thing's for sure – nobody ever had an appointment to see Dave because their life was going great. Kind of tragic, really.

I've discovered that the best way to tag a wall and get away with it is to look calm, cool and totally relaxed, like you have every right in the world to have a spray can in your hand and a piece of brand-new graffiti art in front of you. Often, people will give you a puzzled look, like you can't really be serious, but mostly they will carry on walking. In London, people don't go looking for trouble.

Even so, I don't often have the bottle to make a hit in broad daylight. It's five, and the street is busy, but Dave kind of got to me a little bit and I want to have the last word. The last picture, even.

I sit down on the steps of the Clapham Youth Outreach Centre, rooting around in my bag for some paint. I mean, you have to be prepared, don't you? In case of emergencies.

I watch the people go by for a minute or two, shoppers and workers and schoolkids, and then I turn to face the dull brown doorway behind me, shake the can and start to spray.

It's an old red can and it leaks a little on to my fingers, but that's OK. I'm not trying to hide anything. It doesn't take more than a minute. A fuzzy little heart shape, two dots for eyes and round, cartoon ears. A nose and whiskers. A mouse – my mark.

Nobody stops me, nobody shouts at me, nobody reports me to the police. I put the lid on my spray can, stand up and stroll along to the chippy on Clapham High Street, smiling.

There is nothing quite as good as hot chips drenched in salt and vinegar and tomato ketchup, especially eaten straight from the paper with paint-stained fingers. I'm halfway along the street and halfway through my chips when a small, scruffy, skinny dog appears at my heels. He trots alongside, looking up at me with liquid brown eyes. He's a grubby white colour with a black patch over one eye, like a small pirate, with a filthy red neckerchief tied round his neck in place of a collar. He's after my chips.

'Hey, pal,' I say, offering the dog one perfect, golden chip. He leaps up and takes it from my fingers, fast and graceful, and I swear I can see him grinning.

I like dogs. I used to have one, once – well, she wasn't mine, exactly, but still. Long time ago now. This dog is smaller, smoother and much, much dirtier. He looks like he hasn't eaten in a week, so I feed him chip after chip as we walk along the pavement together. Then all the chips are finished, and the dog's grin slips. He looks desolate.

'No more,' I explain, scrunching the greasy paper into a ball and chucking it at the nearest bin. I miss. The scrunched-up chip paper lands in the gutter, and a gust of wind steers it out into the road. Like a flash, the dog is after it, ducking between a couple of slow-moving cars.

'No!' I shout. 'Come back! Here, boy!'

Time slows down, the way it sometimes does in dreams or on TV. The dog is in the middle of the road. A motorcyclist brakes and swerves to avoid him. My heart thumps, and I stick my fingers in my mouth and whistle, the way my dad taught me once, a long, ear-splitting call, surprisingly loud.

A girl passing by on a bicycle turns to look at me, her hair flying out behind her in golden-brown corkscrew curls. She's the cool girl, the cute girl, from Dave's office. Her startled eyes are green and slanted, like a cat.

The next second she lands in a heap on the pavement in front of me, the bike beneath her. Spreadeagled on the flagstones, under the spinning bicycle wheel, is the small white dog with the pirate patch.

'Omigod, omigod, I didn't see it!' the girl is wailing. 'It just ran right out in front of me . . .'

She drags the bike to one side, and I drop to my knees beside the little pirate dog. He takes a shallow, gasping breath like he's just hanging on by a thread, then his eyes flutter closed and he lies absolutely still.

I think I've killed him.

Some days have disaster printed all over them, right from the start – quite a few of my days, actually. This one, though, is an all-time low. I reach out and touch the dirty, matted fur of the little pirate dog. My fingers are stained with red paint from the spray can, which makes me look like a murderer.

Beneath my palm I feel the faint quiver of a heartbeat. The dog gives a dramatic sigh and his eyes flutter open. I take a deep breath in, weak with relief.

'I am so, sooooooo sorry!' the bicycle girl is saying. 'You just totally spooked me with that whistle. I took my eyes off the road for, like, one millisecond, and the next thing . . .' A fat, salty tear slides down her cheek.

'S'OK,' I tell her. 'Don't cry. He's alive, see?'

Her misty green eyes connect with mine for a moment. She looks younger now, less confident, wiping her eyes on the back of a blazer sleeve and smudging her eyeliner.

A small crowd has gathered around us. We are blocking the pavement, a fallen bike, a green-eyed girl, a dog at death's door and me.

People lean in around us, helping the girl to her feet, checking the bike over. 'All right, love?' a woman with a pushchair asks the girl. 'Not hurt, are you?'

'I'm fine,' the girl says shakily. 'But the little dog . . .'

'A stray, by the look of him,' says the pushchair woman.

'Best phone the council,' someone else suggests. 'They'll take him away, put him out of his misery . . .'

'Out of his misery?' the bicycle girl splutters. 'You can't!'

They can, though. They're people in a hurry, on their way back from bigshot city jobs or busy shopping trips, home to their perfect little families. They don't have time for this. I keep my palm flat against the warm, dirty-white fur of the little pirate dog, just above his heart. It keeps on beating.

'He's not a stray, OK?' I say, calmly but clearly. 'He's mine. So if you all just want to push off . . .'

'Well!' The crowd around us take a tiny step back. One by one, they edge off along the street, muttering about ungrateful kids and dangerous, flea-bitten mongrels.

We've been abandoned.

The girl looks furious. 'What's wrong with people?' she howls. 'Don't they care?'

'Not especially.' I take off my hoodie, wrap the injured dog in it and stand up carefully, holding the bundle close. 'So what? I don't need them.' I stride off along the pavement, and the girl grabs her bike and follows, weaving in and out of the passing shoppers.

Great. A posh girl in a scary school uniform, trailing along behind me.

I look down at the face of the little pirate dog, pressed flat against my chest. His eyes are closed again, his grin fixed and rigid. His heartbeat is steady beneath my palm, but still, I walk a little faster.

'Where are you going, anyway?' the girl asks. 'If you're looking for the nearest vet, you've missed the turning. It was just back there.'

I stop abruptly, frowning. She's right – I have no idea where I'm going. 'OK. Sorry.' I try for a smile. 'Show me. Please?'

The girl wheels round and turns down to the left, and I follow.

'Is he really your dog?' she wants to know. 'I thought he was a stray too.'

I sigh. 'He's mine now, anyhow. Someone has to look out for him.'

'He might be lost, though,' she points out. 'Someone could be looking for him right now, wondering if he's OK.'

I hold the dog tighter. I don't think there's anyone out there worrying about him, somehow. He's small and skinny and sad, like a ghost-dog. He looks like he lives on the streets, getting by on his wits, chasing chip papers, stealing scraps. He doesn't look loved.

'What're you gonna call him?' the girl wants to know. 'He needs a name.'

'I'll think of one,' I say.

'How about Chip?' she offers. 'Or Patch, or Scruff? Hey, I don't even know your name, do I? Mine's Cat.'

'You're kidding, right?' I say.

'No – Cat, short for Catrin, but only my parents call me that. Cat is better.'

I laugh out loud.

'It's not that bad!' she says, huffily. 'What's yours, anyway?'

'It's . . . well, it's a nickname, really, but everybody calls me it, ever since I was little. It's . . .'

'Yeah?'

'Mouse.'

Laughter explodes from her soft, pink mouth like

the fizz from a can of Coke. 'Mouse?' she snorts. 'Mouse?'

I crack a grin. 'Well, it says Martin on my birth certificate, but no one ever, ever calls me that,' I say. 'Except my teachers and stuff, when they're trying to be snotty.'

'So why Mouse?' she wants to know.

I shrug. 'Mum says it's because I was small and quick and quiet. Or maybe because I have mousy hair and a serious addiction to cheese and chocolate. Either way, I've been stuck with it all my life.'

'Cat and Mouse,' she says, grinning. 'That's cool!'

The skinny little stray is stretched out on the examining table, eyelids fluttering. His coat looks dull and grey under the bright lights, and his ribs stick out like the keys on a xylophone. The vet says he'll keep him in, do some X-rays, run some tests.

'It's not just the accident,' the vet says, frowning. 'He's in very poor condition.'

'I haven't had him long,' I say. 'He was a stray, before. He just came up to me in the street.'

'About twenty minutes ago,' Cat chips in, and I roll my eyes up to the ceiling.

'Ah,' says the vet. 'That makes sense. He's very weak and thin, and in shock, obviously. This leg is quite swollen – the X-rays will tell whether it's a break or a sprain. Overall, I'd say he's been lucky.'

This is one of the reasons I find it hard to believe in luck. A small, scruffy, half-starved dog gets squashed by a bicycle, and I'm meant to be grateful because it wasn't a motorbike or a bin lorry?

'Lucky?' I echo. 'Yeah, right.'

As I speak, the little pirate dog pricks up his ears, raises his head and looks at me intently. His mouth twitches into a shaky grin.

'Lucky?' I repeat, and the little dog beats his tail against the examining table like it's Christmas or something. I turn to Cat. 'See that?' I tell her. 'That's his name. Lucky!'

'Yeah?' she says. 'Well. He probably needs all the luck he can get.'

I stroke Lucky's ears softly, and he sighs and lowers his head again, still grinning. 'So when can I collect him?' I ask. 'Take him home?'

The vet looks puzzled. 'He's a stray – don't feel you have to take him. I'll ring the dog's home, once I've fixed him up a bit. They'll look after him, see if he can be re-homed.'

'No chance,' I say. 'Like I said, he's mine.'

The vet scratches his head. 'That's very commendable, of course,' he says. 'If you're serious, you could call back tomorrow afternoon, see how he is. Take some time to think about it.'

'Don't need to think about it,' I tell him. 'I'll be here.'

'We both will,' Cat says.

'You're certain you can offer him a good home?' the vet presses, looking at me doubtfully. 'Your family won't object?'

It depends what his idea of a good home is, of course. The ninth floor of a high-rise on the Eden Estate might not be exactly what he has in mind.

'I'm certain,' I say. 'And my mum'll be fine with it.'

'It's not quite that simple,' the vet says. 'The dog's home would normally pay his vet's bill, but if you take him, that bill becomes your responsibility. It won't be cheap.'

My heart sinks to the bottom of my battered Converse trainers. Money? It feels like a ransom demand.

'You're saying I can't get him back until I cough up a wad of cash?' I demand. 'What are you? A kidnapper or a vet?'

'Is money a problem?' he asks, and I want to punch him.

'No problem at all,' Cat cuts in, smoothly. 'We'll pay. Thank you for all your help! See you tomorrow!'

She grabs my arm and drags me to the door. I crane my head round for a last glimpse of Lucky, but his eyes are closed now, his breathing slow and steady. He doesn't even know he's been kidnapped.

'What are you on?' Cat hisses, the minute we get out the door. 'You can't go around insulting people like that. We'll get the money, OK?'

'How?' I want to know. 'I have 73p to my name.'

'Rich and good-looking, huh?' she jokes, and her green eyes are laughing. If I didn't know better, I'd think she was flirting with me, but posh schoolgirls don't flirt with kids like me. Do they?

'I'll get the money,' she says. 'Easy. I'll meet you here tomorrow afternoon, yeah? What time?'

I think of Lucky, lying there on the examining table, waiting to be ransomed. 'Half nine?' I suggest. 'Ten?'

Cat laughs. 'OK . . . so that's, like, early afternoon, huh?'

I look at her blazer, her tartan pleated skirt. She'll be in school at ten, obviously, studying French irregular verbs or rainfall in the Kalahari desert, or whatever they do at those posh places. She's not excluded, like me. 'Too early?' I ask, curling my lip. 'Gonna be in trouble at school?'

'No, no . . . but d'you think the vet will have had time to run all his tests and stuff?' She's unchaining her bike from the railings, wheeling it to the kerb. Any minute now she'll cycle right out of my life, and I'm kidding myself if I think she'll turn up tomorrow with a handful of cash.

'Mouse?' she prompts.

I scowl, because there's no way I want her to see how I'm feeling. I find a dog, a funny little

21

pirate dog. I give him a chip and the next thing I know he gets squashed flat by a bicycle, and it's all my fault. OK, I got him to the vet, but I can't get him back without a miracle or a handout. I look at Cat from behind my fringe, trying for a smile, but she's not fooled.

'Ten o'clock then,' she says, pulling her beret down, flicking a curl from her face.

'I just want to know he got through the night OK, y'know?' I tell her. 'It was my fault, wasn't it? With the chip paper and the whistle and everything. I feel responsible.'

'You were trying to help him,' she says. 'We're in it together.'

I like the idea of that. 'OK,' I tell her. 'Thanks.'

She still doesn't move, just looks at me with those big green eyes until I think I might forget how to breathe. I tilt my chin and stare right back, scuffing the pavement with the toe of my trainers.

'Look, Mouse,' she says, eventually. 'We haven't got all night. Are you walking me home, or what?'

Actually, she cycles and I run along the pavement beside her, grinning all over my face. We cut across the park and turn into a quiet, tree-lined street. Cat slows a little, freewheeling, studying me. 'How old are you, anyhow?' she asks.

I think about lying, but I'm small and skinny, so there's not much point. 'Fourteen,' I tell her. 'Year Nine.'

'Me too!' she grins. 'Got a girlfriend?'

My heart thumps. 'Not right now.'

Not ever, unless you count Neela Rehman, who dated me for two whole days back in Year Five, in the days when dating just involved lots of smiling and sharing your Mars bar at playtime. I have a sneaky feeling that might have been the attraction. On the third day, I had no money for a Mars bar, and Neela dumped me. She said she'd fallen in love with that blonde-haired guy off *Blue Peter*, but I saw her later in the week, batting her eyes at Liam Gilligan, who had a bag of chocolate caramels.

'OK,' Cat says. 'Good.'

I grin. 'Yeah? You interested?'

'Might be,' she says. 'Might not. I'll think about it.'

So will I. Sheesh, I'll probably dream about it too.

'How about school?' Cat wants to know. 'Don't you just hate it?'

I think of Green Vale Comprehensive, with its eight-foot fences topped with razor wire, its blank, grey, crumbling buildings. It looks more like a detention centre than a school, or a prisoner-of-war camp left over from the Second World War. My mate Fitz once found an ancient, yellow-paged history textbook held together with sellotape, with his grandad's name in the front, dated 1971. Seriously.

'I go to Green Vale Comp,' I tell her. 'It's a dump.'

Her eyes shine. 'Isn't that the place where the kids carry knives in the corridor and they can't get the teachers to stay for more than a week?'

'Uh? No, no, you're way out. The kids carry iPods and most of the teachers have been there since the Dark Ages. Seriously. It's got a bad reputation, though, I guess.'

'I wish I went somewhere cool like that,' Cat sighs. 'I want fun and excitement, not netball and maths tests and diagrams of the digestive system.'

'You wouldn't like Green Vale,' I tell her. 'Trust me. Fun and excitement are not on the timetable.'

'They would be if I was there,' she says.

That makes me smile. We stop in front of a tall, Victorian terraced house with climbing roses around the front door. 'So,' she says. 'Coming in?'

She wheels her bike through the gate and up the little path, turning her key in the lock. Me, I'm still stranded on the pavement trying to take in the shiny blue front door with a stained-glass picture of a sunrise, the bay windows, the way the red-and-yellow brickwork has been arranged to make a pattern all around the doorway. I count the windows going up. Three storeys.

'It's OK,' Cat says over her shoulder. 'Dad works late on a Thursday, and Mum's at her yoga class.'

Inside, the house smells of freshly ground coffee and furniture polish, and I take a deep breath, letting it all sink in. The Eden Estate smells like burnt tyres and pee in the lifts, and that's on a good day. There's a full-length mirror in the hallway, and I catch a glimpse of a wide-eyed kid with a dipping emo fringe, stripy top and skinny jeans. The back of my hair, razored short, is sticking up in clumps like I just spent the night in a hedge. I look shifty, guilty, awkward. I look like trouble.

I haven't a clue what Cat sees in me.

She leans her bike against an antique bookshelf stuffed with more books than I've ever seen, then kicks off her shoes and pads through to the kitchen. 'Drink?' she says.

The kitchen is almost as big as our whole flat. Cat's pouring us fresh orange juice from a fridge the size of a wardrobe. I can't stop staring. I peer into the half-open dishwasher, switch the retro radio CD on and then off again, and sniff at the big vase of roses in the middle of the kitchen table. Then I fling myself down on the big red sofa, bouncing up and down.

'Who has a settee in their kitchen?' I ask, amazed. 'And a telly?'

'Well, we do. Obviously.'

I shake my head. How come some people have so much?

'Knew you were a rich kid,' I say at last.

Cat looks defensive. 'Not rich,' she argues. 'Not really. Rich people live in stately homes and have their own private jets, don't they? They wear designer clothes and jewels at the breakfast table. We're not rich, but we're OK, I suppose. Mum and Dad have good jobs.'

I open a cupboard and find glass jars filled with

funny shapes of pasta, tins of Italian tomatoes, jars of things I've never heard of in my life. I try the fridge, which is stuffed with green salad and Greek yoghurt and weird salami sausages and stinky cheese. 'What are they?' I ask, doubtfully, sniffing at a bowl of what looks like small, shiny animal droppings.

'Black olives,' Cat says. 'Try one.'

'Urghhh!' I have to spit it out into my hand. Cat's family must be loaded. You'd think they'd be able to afford Coke and oven chips and plain old orange cheese, and a rug for the floorboards that isn't threadbare in the middle. Still, I guess they like all that stuff. The rug is probably ancient and valuable, woven in Afghanistan by tribes of nomadic goatherds or something.

'You're rich,' I tell her. 'Don't kid yourself.'

'It's not my fault!' Cat says. 'I didn't ask for middle-class, *Guardian*-reading parents, did I? Everything has to be organic and fairly traded and politically correct. It drives me mad!'

I look out of the kitchen window on to a small garden, lit up in a pool of light. I try to imagine Lucky rooting around the neat flower beds and the green velvet lawn, lifting his leg to pee against the rustic bird table. I can't. My mum would love a patch of garden like this – she'd have the whole thing bursting with colour, dig up the lawn to grow vegetables, train apple trees and jasmine all around the walls.

'I hate this place,' Cat says, her green eyes dark with feeling, and I wonder how she can hate something that seems like heaven to me.

'Swap you then,' I tell her. 'Any day. Life's one big lucky dip, isn't it? You got something cool wrapped in shiny paper, I got the sawdust from the bottom of the barrel.'

She laughs. 'Sawdust? Yeah, right. It can't be that bad. What, d'you live in a cardboard box or something?'

'High-rise block, Eden Estate,' I say bleakly. 'Ninth floor.'

'Wow!' she breathes, which isn't exactly the reaction I was expecting.

Everyone's heard of the Eden Estate – it's a rabbit warren of crumbling high-rise blocks just five minutes walk from here. It might as well be a whole different planet. It's in the paper just about every week. Joyriding, drug dealing, mugging, vandalism – it all happens where I live. At night you can see the helicopters circling round above, like noisy vultures, their searchlights raking through the dark.

'I've never met anyone who lived there before,' Cat says, her eyes shining. 'Cool.'

I roll my eyes. The Eden Estate is not cool – it's a hole, a delapidated, bottom-of-the-pile dumping ground for people who have nowhere else to go. Half the flats are boarded up and derelict, the rest are damp and scummy and falling to bits. People don't choose to live there – they move in until something better comes along, and then they get stuck. It drags them down.

There's a small, stubborn part of me that's proud of the place, though. I've lived there since I was eight years old, and I've survived – just about. Eden made me streetwise, made me tough. It's a mess – but at least it's my mess.

'It's OK,' I tell her. 'Not cool, but you can get by.'

'So where do you live, exactly?' Cat presses.

'Nightingale House, ninth floor,' I say, then stop short. 'Don't even think about visiting, OK? It's dodgy if you don't know what you're doing. I mean it, Cat.'

'You worry too much!' She slides on to the sofa next to me, looking at me closely like I'm some fascinating specimen of insect she has under a magnifying glass.

'I like you, Mouse,' she says. 'You're funny. And cute.'

I try not to panic as she slides an arm along the back of the sofa, because things never got this far with Neela Rehman, back in Year Five, and I'm way out of my depth.

Out in the hallway, the front door slams and Cat jumps across the room like she's just been scalded.

'Cat?' calls a woman's voice. 'Is that you? I thought you'd still be at drama club! I forgot my yoga mat, so . . . oh! Who's this?'

A small, striking black woman stands in the kitchen doorway, eyes narrowed. She looks at me like I'm a lump of chewing gum stuck to her shoe, or maybe something worse.

'Hello. I'm Mia, Catrin's mum. And you are . . .?'

'Just leaving,' I say, standing up quickly.

'His name is Ben,' Cat says quickly. 'Ben . . . Smith.'

I grin. I've never heard of Ben Smith, but he's obviously more acceptable to Cat's mum than I am.

'Well, Ben.' She looks me up and down, eyes lingering on my bird's-nest hair and trailing bootlaces. I feel like I should grab a comb and start saving up for a suit right away. 'I take it you're at drama club together?' she asks.

'Er . . .'

'That's right,' Cat says. 'We're working on a new play, in pairs . . .'

'Oh? What play?' She's looking right at me with dark, suspicious eyes, and my mind goes blank.

'*Shrek?*' I suggest.

'*Hamlet*,' Cat corrects me, but her mum is unimpressed.

'It's, like, a postmodern version of Shakespeare,' Cat gabbles. 'A sort of fusion of two opposing styles. All the main characters are played by trolls and donkeys . . .'

'Yeah,' I cut in, before she has a chance to dig herself in any deeper. 'It was cool. Anyway, Mrs . . . erm, Mia. I have to go now. Nice meeting you!'

'What about your play?' she calls after me, an edge of sarcasm in her voice, but I'm off, hands in pockets, sloping up the garden path, on my way home to a whole different planet.

It's ten past ten, and still there's no sign of Cat. I shouldn't have expected it, really, not after last night. I could see what her mum thought – she looked at me and she smelt trouble, the way other people might smell Tesco Value Shampoo.

Cat'll be in school right now, telling her stuck-up mates about the boy she met from the Eden Estate who'd never even seen an olive before. Me, I'm sitting on the steps outside the vet's with 73p to my name. I have a plan, though. I'm going to go in, see how Lucky is, then ask the vet to give me more time to pay the bill. I'll wash his car for him, or clean out his hamster cages, mop the floors. Whatever it takes. How much can a vet's bill actually be?

'Hey!' Cat is waving from the other side of the road. I fight back the grin that's threatening to take over my face, and get up lazily, hands in pockets.

She's not in school uniform today, and she looks at least sixteen. She's wearing a short black

32

sweater-dress over footless tights, a studded belt hanging slantwise over her hips. A black beanie hat is pulled down over her corkscrew hair. She crosses the road and comes towards me, and I fall for her honey-brown skin and emerald eyes all over again. I don't want her to know that, though.

'What took you so long?' I ask. 'D'you think of a way to pay the bill?'

'Of course,' she says. 'I told you, didn't I? Not a problem.'

We go inside, and the vet lets us go through to the back where Lucky is asleep in a big metal cage. He looks like he's in prison.

'He looks thinner,' I say, but apparently Lucky ate a good meal last night, and slept well.

'He's doing fine,' the vet says. 'We'll do the X-rays later, and fix that leg up. He should be ready to collect at evening surgery, if you're still sure . . .'

'I'm sure.'

'And the bill?'

I don't blame him for being suspicious. I wouldn't trust us, either. 'We can pay now, if you like,' Cat says, bringing out a roll of money.

The vet raises an eyebrow, taps something into his computer, then prints out a bill and hands it over. 'I'm charging you for the X-rays and the medication,' he says. 'But not the overnight stay.

Just don't tell anyone – they'll think I'm a total pushover.'

'Thanks!' I grin, and then I look at the bill and see that it's still £108, so that wipes the smile off my face pretty quickly. Cat doesn't even flinch, just hands over the money with a smile.

'See ya later, kid,' she says to Lucky, and I wink at him, because you can't stroke a dog through the bars of a cage. We promise to be back by seven o'clock surgery.

That's a lot of time to kill, but Cat's ready for the challenge. Twenty minutes later we are squashed together on a tube train, hurtling through the London Underground on the way to Covent Garden.

'It's not like I normally skive off school,' she tells me. The woman opposite gives her a frowny look, and she lowers her voice.

'I'm doing this for you, Mouse,' she goes on. 'Because you're worried about Lucky and you need cheering up. Besides, I have a French test this afternoon.'

'You're all heart,' I say.

'I know. Anyhow, you're bunking off too.'

I laugh. 'I'm not skiving, I'm excluded.'

The woman opposite chokes on her takeaway coffee, but Cat looks entranced. 'Wow!' she says. 'What did you do?'

I lower my voice to a whisper. 'I tagged the wall of my school gym with eight different colours of spray paint.'

'Unreal,' Cat breathes. 'What made you do it?'

That question again. There are a million reasons, all of them true. I thought it would be cool, I thought it would be funny. I wanted to show my art teacher, a wrinkled dinosaur in a tweed suit, that I could draw.

'I was bored,' I say, because that's as good a reason as any.

School – it's enough to make anyone turn vandal. The lessons are pointless and dull, day after day, week after week, year after year, so that in the end you just about lose the will to live. You start dreaming about rebellion, about locking the teachers into the school canteen and force-feeding them lumpy custard while you build a bonfire on the playing fields with every exercise book, every exam paper in the school. Anything, really – anything to kill the boredom, because nothing ever happens at Green Vale Comp.

And then it did, and for five whole minutes I was a king, a hero. In a quiet kind of way, because nobody knew it was me – until Chan noticed the paint on my fingers and pointed out the spelling mistakes and told me to get out of there. I was on my way out of the door, feeling like Van Gogh with a paint can, when Mr Brown grabbed me by the collar and it was all over, my moment of glory, just like that.

'So they excluded you,' Cat says. 'Did the police get involved?'

'No, Dave spoke up for me and the school agreed not to press charges,' I say. 'I had to promise never to do it again.'

'And will you?'

'No chance,' I tell her. 'Caused too much trouble.'

'Yeah?' She sneaks a look at my fingers. They are scrubbed and clean, with just the faintest rim of red around the fingernails.

'Your graffiti days are done?' she checks.

'Definitely.'

'So what about the door of the Youth Outreach Unit, yesterday?' she asks, triumphant. 'A little mouse face, in the corner. I saw it when I was unlocking my bike, and I knew it hadn't been there when I went in. That was you, wasn't it? Had to be.'

'Caught red-handed,' I say.

6 COVENT GARDEN

We get off the tube at Covent Garden, take the lift up to the surface and emerge on to a chaotic street stuffed with tourists and street performers. I'm still trying to take it all in when a tall, dark-haired bloke walks by, flashing us a sparkly-white grin.

'I think I know him,' I say.

Cat rolls her eyes. 'Of course you know him,' she hisses. 'That's Robbie Williams! Don't stare – he'll think you're a fan or something!'

'This place is crazy!'

'You've been here before, right?' she asks. 'You must have!'

I shrug. 'I've heard of it, but . . .'

'Typical,' she says. 'We live right here in London, but when do we ever really explore? That's why skiving off, once in a while, is so cool. You can get to be a tourist for a day. That's what we're going to do!'

We've only gone a few paces when Cat stops, mesmerized by a guy who has sprayed himself silver from head to toe. He stands as still as a statue, while Japanese tourists with fancy cameras take shot after shot.

'Even his nostrils are silver,' she marvels. 'And inside his ears. Do you think he'll ever get it off?'

I think of my own red-stained fingers, and hope that the silver guy used face paint, not aerosol cans. Does painting yourself silver count as an act of mindless vandalism? Probably not. 'Awesome,' Cat says, dropping a pound coin into a bucket at the silver guy's feet. He springs to life, taking a sweeping bow, offering her a long-stemmed silver flower. She takes the flower and blows the silver guy a kiss, laughing.

We move on into the main square. There's a junk market inside a huge, wide building and an outdoor market too, rows of stalls crammed into the courtyard space between the shops. To our right, crowds of people lounge on rows of steps, watching a troupe of acrobats doing handsprings and human pyramids.

Cat is already cruising the stalls, sniffing handmade soaps, tasting samples of fudge. When I approach, the stallholders blank me and move their samples out of reach. Typical. I stand back, admiring Cat's confidence as she chats up the stallholder on a stand selling handmade chocolates, when the breath catches in my throat.

Quickly, carelessly, as the stallholder turns to speak to another customer, Cat picks up a large, ribbon-wrapped box of chocolates and slips it into her bag. It happens so fast I can't quite believe what I've seen. I frown, waiting for her to hand over the money, but she doesn't. She just pops one last sample chocolate into her mouth and moves on through the crowd.

My new friend, the shoplifter.

OK, I knew she was trouble – she wouldn't have been in Dave's office otherwise – but I didn't know what flavour of trouble. There are any amount of reasons why you might end up seeing a social worker. Your life goes out of shape. Your family might be messed up, or missing, or ill. Maybe you're in trouble at school, or with the police. Maybe you steal things.

I used to do it myself, years ago. I took things from shops – sweets, pop, crisps – sometimes because I was hungry, sometimes because I just didn't know any better. I learnt in the end though, and these days I don't take stuff that doesn't belong to me, no matter how tempting it might be.

Cat does. I'm surprised how much this bugs me. I'm sitting on the steps watching the acrobats, when she tracks me down.

'Where d'you go?' she asks. 'I was looking everywhere!'

She sits down beside me. In front of us, one of the performers is juggling beanbags with ribbon tails attached. They make rainbow arcs of colour as they fly through the air. 'Good, huh?' she says.

I blow air out between my lips, unimpressed. 'My dad was a juggler,' I say without thinking. 'He juggled with fire. Better than this lot, by miles.'

'Yeah? What does he do now?'

I shrug. 'Dunno. He never lived with Mum and me – not since I was about two anyhow. I stayed with him one summer, back when I was seven, when Mum was ill. I thought I'd get to know him, but I didn't get the chance. He took off and left me, went to India with his girlfriend and promised to send for me. He never did.'

'Oh, Mouse, I'm sorry.'

Stupid, stupid, stupid. That's what happens when you let the past leak out from the boxes in your head where you've packed it carefully away – people look at you with pity in their eyes, and that's a look I've had enough of. Too late now, though.

'I'm not sorry,' I say, fiercely. 'He was a waste of space. I hardly knew him, y'know?'

Cat looks confused. She has a normal family, after all, even if they are posh. I bet her dad was never a juggler. I bet he never even thought of ditching his kid to run off to India. How could she understand?

'This'll put a smile on your face,' she says gently, taking out the handmade chocolates in their ribbon-wrapped box. 'They're for you.'

'No thanks,' I say.

Her face falls. 'Why not? I thought you'd be pleased!'

'Did you?'

'Mouse, what's up?' she asks. 'What did I do?'

'It's what you didn't do,' I tell her. 'You didn't pay.'

A pink flush darkens Cat's honey-brown cheeks, and her eyes flicker with doubt. 'Of course I did. I –'

'Cat, don't lie to me,' I say. 'I can't stand liars. OK? I saw you.'

'I thought . . . look, it was just a laugh! These stalls must get stuff nicked all the time. They expect it.'

'That doesn't make it right!' I tell her. 'Look, Cat, I don't want you nicking stuff for me, OK? I don't like it.'

Cat pulls a face. 'Sorr-eee,' she says.

'I don't get it,' I say. 'I know you're trouble – you wouldn't have been in Dave's office, otherwise. I'm not judging you, Cat, but seriously, you don't have to steal. You have a nice house, what looks like an OK family. You handed over a hundred quid for that crazy vet's bill, and you didn't even blink. You don't need to steal.'

'I don't even know why I did it. I'm sorry . . .'

'It's wrong. You have to put them back.'

'Mouse, are you crazy?' she yelps. 'I'm sorry I took them, OK? I didn't mean to annoy you. But seriously, no way –'

I grab the chocolates and slide them under my jacket, and walk off into the crowd. When I reach the chocolate stall, I try to look casual, pretending to choose between the prettily arranged boxes. The stallholder watches me, stony-faced. When she turns to serve a customer, I slip the stolen chocolates back on to the tabletop.

'Hey!' the stallholder yells. 'I saw that! What are you doing?'

That wasn't meant to happen. The stallholder is screeching and shaking her fist at me, which seems a little harsh, considering I was replacing a box of chocolates, not nicking one. I don't hang around to argue – I break into a run, elbowing my way through the crowds.

'Stop! Thief!' she shouts, and people turn to stare.

Suddenly Cat appears at my side. She wraps cool brown fingers round my own and tugs me into a quiet side street. We run through on to The Strand, plunge into a crowd of shoppers crossing the busy road. 'There he is!' a voice yells behind me, and Cat drags me down another side street, past walls of shiny plate glass, queues of glossy black cars. She slows to a stroll, tosses her head back and winks at a hotel porter in a fancy coat with a big top hat. He holds open a door and we walk through, and behind us the shouts and hassles fade away.

My feet sink into thick carpet as Cat leads me past a bank of plush sofas and shiny potted palms. 'What is this place?' I ask her.

'The Savoy Hotel,' she whispers.

'Cat!' I hiss at her. 'What are you playing at? We can't –'

'We can! Tea for two, please,' she says, smiling at a stern-faced waiter, who melts visibly. 'Lapsang souchong?'

That last bit sounds like Japanese to me, but the waiter beams at Cat. 'Certainly, Miss,' he says. 'We're not serving our traditional afternoon tea just yet, but I'm sure we can arrange something. If the young man would just remove his hat? We have a dress code, you know.'

He scans my skinny jeans as if looking for holes and rips, but finds nothing. I take off my beanie and he slides his eyes over my chin-length fringe with a despairing sigh. 'Over here, please.' The waiter shows us to a couple of armchairs arranged beneath a big gilt mirror, and we sit down, sinking into the plush velvet.

'We came here for Mum's birthday, last year,'

Cat whispers to me. 'You just have to act confident.'

Acting confident is not an option, but I do my best not to faint in terror as the waiter delivers a silver tray laden with bone-china cups and teapot. Cat grabs a mini-sieve and pours her tea, dropping in a couple of sugar lumps with a pair of silver tongs. Me, I'm all fingers and thumbs. My hands shake as I lift the teacup. I slop hot tea across my jeans and have to mop it up with a thick linen napkin the size of a small bath towel. 'Relax,' Cat whispers. 'Just enjoy it!' I gulp my tea, spilling puddles of it every time a waiter stalks past, but Cat takes her time, nibbling biscuits and pouring herself a second cup.

'Am I forgiven?' she asks, wiping the crumbs from round her lips with the tip of her pink tongue.

'Forgiven?' I hiss. 'You're crazy. You'll get us arrested. Deported, maybe. The police are probably on their way right now . . .'

The waiter glides over and slips the bill discreetly on to a side plate. One thing's for sure, tea at The Savoy is not going to be cheap. 'Gonna do a runner?' I ask as Cat unfolds the bill, and she kicks my shin under the table. I have a feeling that anyone trying to escape without paying would be shot, quickly and silently, with a non-fatal poison dart. You'd wake up in the hotel kitchen, chained to a dishwasher, washing bone-china teacups for the rest of your life.

Cat calls over the waiter, hands him several crisp notes and tells him to keep the change. She hooks her arm through mine and we walk out of a side door, heads high. Cat starts to laugh, and suddenly the whole situation seems so weird and wonderful that I'm laughing too. The doorman doesn't seem to mind, and tips his hat to us with a grin. We head down towards the river, walking hand in hand, looking across the water at the London Eye as it turns slowly in the thin October sun.

'Ever been on the London Eye?' Cat asks.

'No, never.'

'Let's do it then!'

We run down to where a clump of tourists are queuing to get on a river cruiser. Some of them are French teenagers, being herded together by a couple of teachers. Cat edges right into the centre of the crowd, pulling me after her until we are surrounded by French kids.

'*Comment ça va?*' she asks me, in a perfect French accent.

'What?'

'*Oh, mon ami,*' Cat says. '*Ma petit souris.* Shhh!' She puts a finger to my lips, silencing me. The crowd edges forward, and we are carried on to the boat. Nobody asks us for money, or tickets. The

French teachers don't seem to notice they have acquired two extra students.

'Always works,' Cat says, grinning. We stand by the rail and gaze out over the river, the breeze ruffling our hair.

'Sorry about the chocolates,' she says.

'It's OK,' I tell her. 'You're mad, you know?'

'Nah. I'm just trying to take your mind off stuff. Is it working?'

'Might be.'

Later, as we press our noses against the glass of the pod in capsule 17 of the London Eye, Cat takes my hand again. For a moment I forget about the scruffy pirate dog with the injured leg, about Mum and the flats and being excluded, about the stolen chocolates and The Savoy Hotel and the river boat full of French teenagers. I just lean against the glass and look out over the city. It's dusk, and the water looks shimmery and bright, reflecting the glinting lights strung out along the Thames Embankment.

'I could stay here forever,' I tell Cat. 'On top of the world.'

'Me too,' she says, and just for a moment, nothing else matters – nothing at all.

You can't stay on top of the world forever, though. You have to come down, and in the end we did. We took the tube back to Clapham and collected Lucky from the vet, and it turned out that his leg was sprained and not broken, but it was all bandaged up anyhow. He looked more like a pirate dog than ever. All that was missing was the parrot on the shoulder.

I thanked the vet and tucked Lucky under my arm, and the three of us walked along to Cat's house. Time was running too fast, like it always does when you want something to last. We stood at the gate in a little pool of light from the street lamp, and Cat looked at me with her eyes all soft and smiley, like she was waiting for me to kiss her or ask her on a date.

I didn't, though. I knew enough to suss that there'd be no future for a boy from the Eden Estate and a girl like Cat.

We said goodbye and I promised to bring Lucky

round to see her sometime, when he was better, even though we both knew it probably wouldn't happen. And then the front door creaked open and her mum appeared on the steps and called her in, and that was it, over.

When I was eight years old and Mum told me we were moving to the Eden Estate, I thought it would be like paradise. First off, we'd be together again, after almost a whole year of being apart. I'd have been happy wherever we were, but Mum told me we'd be living way up on the ninth floor, with a view clear across London. Our garden would be one big stretch of pure blue sky.

Our block was called Nightingale House. That sounded kind of magical, as if you could fall asleep to the sound of birds singing, but actually it turned out that you fall asleep to the sound of sirens and shouting and people playing their music too loud. Our view was mainly the tower block opposite, but Mum was right, we had our own patch of pure blue sky, and nobody could do much to mess that up, however hard they tried.

Eden Estate is bigger than you'd think, a city inside a city. There are four big blocks, all with wraparound balconies and scabby satellite dishes jutting out awkwardly. There is no colour, no texture except for the peeling layers of grey paint, the endless pebble-dash. The blocks are all called after birds, which was probably some council planner's idea of a joke, because you'd be lucky to catch so much as a one-legged pigeon hanging out around here.

Some nights the place is quiet, almost peaceful, but tonight isn't one of them. There's a smouldering fire in the middle of the pavement, fluttering pages from the *Daily Star* blowing along the kerb like tumbleweed. A shiny Ford Ka sits abandoned in the middle of the road, minus its wheels, one door hanging open as if the driver just nipped out and never returned.

I wonder if Cat would think it was cool? Probably.

Lucky whimpers, sniffing at the air, and I hold him a little closer. He's going to have to get used to this, like I did, but he's a street dog, a survivor. He'll be OK.

We pass a kids' playground where the swings have long since been trashed. A huddle of older teenagers sit crouched on the ancient roundabout, smoking and listening to rap music on a ghetto blaster. 'Hey, Mouse,' one of them calls through the dark, and I wave and keep walking, past Eagle Heights and Skylark Rise.

Little kids on bikes are circling the Phoenix Drop-In, a wooden hut surrounded by a chain-link fence. It's just about the only splash of colour on the whole estate, with its sky-blue walls and fiery spray-paint phoenix mural. Inside the fence is a tiny garden stuffed with bright flowers and veggies and fruit trees trained in fancy patterns along the fence. I did the mural, and Mum does a lot of the gardening stuff – she works at the Phoenix. It's a day centre for recovering drug addicts, so it's not an easy job, but she loves it. She cares.

Outside the lifts in Nightingale House, my mate Chan's little sister and her pals are playing with Barbie dolls. One of the dolls must be Ballerina Barbie, dressed in a tutu and satin ballet shoes. The other is a wild-haired thing in plastic boots and a minidress, covered in felt pen tattoos. Probably Eden Estate Barbie.

The little girls run up to see Lucky, squealing with delight. The lift appears, clanking and sighing its way to the ninth floor, and then it's just a walk along the hallway to flat 114. I pass old Mrs Scully, out with her can of Mr Sheen, polishing her front door in spite of the peeling paint and the fact that it's past eight o'clock at night.

'Hello, dear!' She smiles, and her skin crinkles up so that it looks like a contour map of the Himalayas we once studied in geography, all spidery lines and wrinkles. She looks hard at Lucky. 'Is that my Frankie's dog?'

'No, he's mine, Mrs S.,' I say. 'His name's Lucky.'

'Must need new glasses,' she says, shaking her head. 'Sorry. He's very sweet.'

'Let's hope Mum thinks so,' I say over my shoulder. The doors on either side of our flat are boarded up, but number 114 is painted spray-can red with a graffiti tag of a mouse-face on the concrete floor in place of a doormat.

I hope Mum's going to be OK with this. I didn't mention Lucky to her last night – I wasn't sure how things would turn out. Now, though, it's real. I shrug off my hoodie, wrap Lucky inside it, turn the key in the lock.

'Mum?' I call. She's curled up on a beanbag in the living room, watching TV, surrounded by huge, jungly houseplants that stretch up to the ceiling. The place looks more like Kew Gardens than somebody's flat. The plants are good, though – they hide the damp patches on the wall, the peeling wallpaper.

Mum's small, like me, with mouse-brown hair in an urchin crop, and big grey eyes that always look amazed or happy or hopeful.

'Hi, Mouse,' she says, flashing me a smile. 'Have you eaten? There's pizza in the kitchen. Oh . . . what have you got there?'

I put my hoodie-wrapped parcel down in the

middle of the scratchy nylon carpet. 'A surprise,' I tell her. 'I know I should have asked you first, but . . .'

Lucky sticks his head out of the folds of black fabric, grinning, and Mum's hands fly to her face. She looks horrified. 'Mouse!' she shrieks. 'What the . . . Mouse, what are you doing with Frank Scully's dog?'

A sad, frozen feeling settles in the pit of my stomach. I'd argue, but Mrs Scully's words are still fresh in my ears.

I've been blanking the idea that Lucky might have an owner, but an owner like Frank Scully? That's just too sick. He's one of the estate's small-time crooks, a weasel-faced loser with a drug habit who also happens to be the grandson of the sweet old lady with the Mr Sheen fixation. Scully is bad news.

'Scully's dog?' I echo. 'No way. I didn't know Scully had a dog!'

If he did, surely it would be a Rottweiler or a Staffie. He wouldn't want a skinny little terrier with a pirate patch. Would he?

Mum bites her lip. 'He has a dog now, not much more than a pup,' she tells me. 'And this is it. I recognize the patch over the eye, and the bandana. He brought it into the Phoenix a while ago, told everyone he won it in a card game. Poor thing was starving – I gave it a plate of macaroni cheese.'

Lucky battles his way free of the hoodie and takes a couple of limping steps forward. He looks from me to Mum and back again, but I can't quite meet his eyes.

'Where did you find him?'

'Near Dave's office, yesterday,' I say. 'He got run over by a girl on a bicycle. We got him fixed up – even the vet thought he was a stray!'

'He's not, Mouse. We can't keep him – Scully's not the kind of bloke I'd want as an enemy.'

Nobody would want Scully as an enemy – not many would want him as a friend, either.

'I've been calling him Lucky,' I say. 'Funny, huh? He must be the unluckiest dog in London. How come he was wandering around the streets anyway? How come he was so thin and dirty? That loser won't look after him, Mum, you know he won't!'

Mum looks upset. 'What did the vet say?'

'Just a sprain. He'll be good as new in a few days. If he's properly looked after, that is . . .'

'If,' Mum says.

There's a long silence while Lucky tilts his head to one side and does his best impression of a hungry, homeless, unloved mutt. Mum chews her lip. She's always been a sucker for waifs, strays and lost causes – I can see her struggling to resist Lucky's sad-eyed gaze.

'OK, OK,' she says, at last. 'We'll keep him for a day or two, until his leg's better. Don't go telling everyone – we don't want Scully turning up on the doorstep looking for a fight.'

'Mrs S. recognized him just now,' I admit. 'I thought she was nuts, but obviously not. She said she must need new glasses.'

'How a lovely old lady like that ended up with that thug for a grandson I'll never know,' Mum says. 'Never mind, Mouse. I don't think that'll matter, not if it's just for a couple of days. And it is just for a couple of days, OK?'

'OK.'

Later, wrapped in our fluffiest bath towel and eating pizza, Lucky settles on a big floor cushion under the Swiss cheese plant. He no longer looks as if he's been living in a coal mine.

'Don't get too used to it,' Mum warns him. 'This is temporary.'

Lucky looks up from his pizza crust, grinning, and she ruffles his ears. I reckon she could get attached to him – his grubby bandana is swishing around in the washing machine right now. Everything would be perfect if it wasn't for Frank Scully.

'Scully might be glad to be rid of him,' I think out loud.

'Maybe,' Mum says. 'If we explain it to him gently. The next time he turns up at the Phoenix I'll have a quiet word, see what he says.'

If anyone can talk Scully round, Mum can. She tried to help him years ago, when the Phoenix first opened. He was still in his teens then, on probation for a drugs-related theft, and he came along to the Phoenix every day for a fortnight before his lowlife mates lured him back to a life of crime. Since then, he's been in prison twice, and even his mum and gran have given up on him. I frown. Something, somewhere, doesn't quite add up.

'What's Scully doing hanging around the Phoenix anyway?' I ask. 'He's a dealer, isn't he? Don't tell me he's trying to clean up his act – no way.'

Mum shakes her head. 'Mouse, I know,' she says. 'I don't trust him either. He's been along a few times lately. If he says he wants to change, what can we do? We can't refuse him the chance to try.'

I wince. Letting Scully into the Phoenix is like allowing a fox into your chicken house – asking for trouble. I bet he's only hanging around for a free meal. Or – the thought makes me go cold all over – to push drugs on vulnerable ex-junkies when nobody's looking.

'Don't worry, I'm watching him,' Mum says, as if she can read my mind.

Lucky turns in a circle three times, then settles down to sleep.

'Lucky,' Mum says, thoughtfully. 'Well, let's hope he is.'

My CD alarm crashes into life with My Chemical Romance yelling about the Black Parade. I open one eye, wince and hide under the covers again.

Last year, I had the bright idea of covering up the peeling woodchip wallpaper in my bedroom by using up all the odds and ends of spray paint I had lying around. It looks like an explosion in a paint factory, which is cool most of the time, but first thing in the morning it can be kind of traumatic. All those swirling, clashing colours and patterns are not for the faint-hearted.

A wet nose snuffles against my neck – Lucky. I hug him close and tell him I'll keep him safe from Frank Scully, though I don't have a scooby how. 'I'll think of something,' I promise. 'Trust me.' Lucky sighs and smiles and burrows in under the duvet, and the two of us sleep till midday.

The doors to Jake's workshop are flung wide, with scabby, half-wrecked cars spilling out on to the forecourt. One of them, a rusting Lada, has the bonnet up, and I can see my best friend's trademark baggy jeans as he leans over it, fiddling with spark plugs and bits of wire.

'Hey, Fitz!' I call over, and he comes out from under the bonnet, oil-smeared and grinning.

'Look who it is – the spray-can king of Green Vale Comp!' he says. 'How's it feel to be a juvenile delinquent?'

'You tell me,' I laugh. 'You've had more practice!'

'That's harsh, Mouse,' Fitz replies. 'I'm just misunderstood. I'm a joker, man, yeah? A stink bomb here, a tap left running there, a fire alarm accidentally set off just before the Year Nine exams . . . I'm only acting in the interests of my fellow students.'

'Practically a saint, huh?' I say.

'You got it. You and me, Mouse, we're like silent superheroes, saving the world from boredom, misery and double maths.'

I laugh, leaning up against the Lada.

'Anyway, man, you're busted, right?' Fitz tells me. 'You were seen. Your secret's out!'

'My secret?'

'Don't pretend you don't know. Like I said, you were seen. Jake!' he yells. 'Jake, it's Mouse!'

Jake comes out from the workshop, wiping his

hands on paint-spattered overalls. He's Fitz's dad, although he doesn't look like a dad – he's still pretty young himself. You get the feeling he and Fitz's mum weren't exactly planning a baby, but Fitz came along anyway. Jake wasn't ready to settle down, though. He's never lived with Fitz and his mum and gran, even though he sees Fitz plenty.

It's the kind of cool, matey relationship I always imagined I might have with my dad, only in my case it didn't happen. It's not just that my dad wasn't ready to settle down, he wasn't ready to even live on the same continent as me.

'Come on then, Romeo,' Jake says, flicking me with an oily rag. 'Spill it. Who is she?'

I start to grin. 'Who's who?' I bluff.

'The girlfriend, man!' Fitz bursts out. 'The chick you were holding hands with last night! Jake saw you, Mouse, OK?'

'Comin' out of the tube station,' Jake says. 'I was making a little – ah – delivery, nearby. I waved, but the pair of you were too wrapped up to notice. Young love, eh? Way-hey-hey!'

The two of them smirk and nudge each other, like they just caught me walking along Clapham High Street in lime-green swimming shorts and a pair of flippers.

I hide behind my fringe. 'She's just a friend,' I say.

'Just a friend?' Fitz snorts. 'No, no, Mouse, I'm just a friend. Chan is just a friend. You don't hold hands with us, do you? Nope, this chick is not just a friend!'

'Pretty too,' Jake chips in.

I sigh. 'Yeah, she's cute,' I tell them. 'But she goes to a posh private school and lives up Rivendale Avenue in a house with roses around the door. So even if I did like her, it wouldn't be happening, OK?'

'Why not?' Jake demands. 'So what if she's posh? Shouldn't make any difference, mate. You gotta be confident, get out there, grab the world by the throat.'

'Don't go telling him that,' Fitz argues. 'We'll never hear the last of it. Pass her on to me, man, I'll look after her!'

'In your dreams,' I say, and Fitz just grins.

Jake chucks me a couple of newspapers and a roll of masking tape. 'I've got work to do here,' he tells me. 'You helpin', or not?'

'Might do,' I say. I like helping Jake out, especially if I'm trying to earn some cash, and he always gives me his leftover spray cans, which is cool. 'What needs doing?'

Jake points to a big, blue, shiny four-wheel drive in a corner of the workshop. 'Paint-job,' he says. 'From blue to black – needs masking up. Don't bother with the windows, I'm replacing them anyway – just the chrome and stuff. OK?'

I frown at the four-wheel drive. It looks brand new, and hardly in need of a paint-job, especially one to change the colour. I notice that Jake has taken off the number plates, and he's obviously planning to change the windows too. It crosses my mind that this car may not be strictly legal.

'Whose is it?' I ask, wrapping a wing mirror with newspaper, taping down the edges neatly.

'Let's just say it's for a couple of important local businessmen,' Jake says. 'So do a good job, yeah?'

Fitz pulls a face. On the Eden Estate, businessman translates as drug dealer, and/or crook. Jake is a nice guy, but he has some seriously dodgy friends. He manages to stay out of trouble most of the time, but only just.

Fitz chooses not to talk about his dad's iffy mates, or the fact that some of the resprays and repairs he does at the garage may not be strictly above board, so I ignore it too.

Fitz turns back to his spark plugs. 'How d'you meet her?' he wants to know. 'This posh girl? She got any friends?'

'Like I'd let you loose on her mates!' I tell him. 'As if! I met her in Clapham High Street – she ran over this little dog and landed on the pavement in front of me.'

'She fell for you, man,' Fitz laughs.

'Funny,' I say. 'Like I said, Fitz, this relationship isn't going anywhere. She's posh – different. It wouldn't work out.'

'Who cares?' Fitz says. 'Maybe she wants to slum it a bit!'

Maybe she does, but I don't want to be an experiment in how the other half live. Cat's gorgeous, but she's out of my league. 'We took the dog to the vet's,' I say, masking off the front grille. 'I reckoned it was a stray, so I brought it home.'

Fitz ducks out again from under the bonnet, his face a picture of disgust. 'Let's get this straight,' he says. 'You ditched the girl but kept the dog? Mouse, what's wrong with you?'

'Nothing!' I protest.

'You're crazy,' Fitz declares. 'Seriously.'

I chew my lip. 'Well, maybe I am,' I tell him. 'You'll never guess whose dog it turned out to be? Only Frank Scully's, that's all. How scary is that?'

Fitz blinks. 'Very scary, man,' he says. 'You gave it back, yeah? The dog?'

I turn back to the four-wheel drive, folding and shaping newspaper to the side window, so Fitz can't see my face. 'Not yet,' I admit. 'I mean, I'm going to, when the dog's all better and stuff . . .' As I say this, I know that deep down, I have no intention of ever, ever letting Lucky go back to Frank Scully. I'd sooner hand him over to Cruella de Vil.

'You'd better, man,' Fitz is saying. 'I mean, that guy doesn't have a sense of humour . . .'

A firm hand lands on my shoulder, and I just about jump out of my skin. 'A word of advice, Mouse, mate,' Jake says, and his eyes are serious, his grin long gone. 'You're a good kid. I like you a lot, you know that – so listen. Frank lost his dog a week or so back – probably just ran off, he wasn't exactly treating it well, but he thinks someone stole it. If you found the dog, give it back, Mouse. Don't get on the wrong side of Frank Scully. OK?'

I swallow, hard. 'I'll try not to,' I mutter.

Jake shakes his head, his forehead creased and anxious. 'Try hard,' he says.

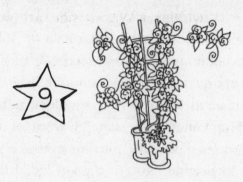

I spend the rest of Saturday worrying about what Jake said, and most of Sunday trying to find a way to tell Mum about it. In the end, I mutter something about Scully thinking his dog's been nicked, and Mum tells me not to stress, she'll talk to Scully if and when he turns up at the Phoenix.

'I can handle him,' she says. A prickle of fear snakes down my back, because I don't think anyone can handle Frank Scully. He's a madman – Jake just about spelled it out for me.

'I don't want Lucky to go back,' I say. 'I like having him around.'

'Me too,' Mum says. 'But he doesn't belong to us. Let's wait and see.'

I'm so jumpy by Monday, when Mum goes back to the Phoenix, I just about fall off my chair when the doorbell chimes out at midday. Lucky starts barking, his tail waving like a propeller, and I grab his muzzle to shut him up in case it's Scully out there, raging mad and swinging a baseball bat.

'Shhh!' I whisper. 'Whose side are you on, anyway?'

I shut him in my bedroom and walk to the door. It's half-term, so the chances are it'll be Fitz or Chan. I open the door a crack and my heart lurches. It's not Fitz, Chan or even Scully. It's a green-eyed girl with honey-coloured skin and a guilty smile, leaning on her bicycle.

'Surprise!' she says.

I'm not surprised, I'm horrified. I've dreamed about Cat for three nights running. I've replayed every word she said to me, every stunt she pulled. She's cool and funny and she has 'trouble' printed right through the middle of her, like 'Blackpool' through a stick of rock, but she doesn't belong on the Eden Estate.

'Cat,' I say. 'You shouldn't be here.'

Her face falls. 'Well, I am,' she tells me. 'Aren't you pleased to see me?'

'No! Well – yes. But . . .'

'Mouse, aren't you going to let me in?'

Defeated, I stand back as she wheels the bike inside and leans it against a wall of hanging coats. Lucky has escaped from the bedroom and goes crazy, circling her, jumping up, smothering her with kisses when she bends to make a fuss of him. 'Oh, he's all clean and happy!' she says. 'His bandana's good as new! At least he's glad to see me . . .'

'We both are,' I say grudgingly. 'I suppose. I just didn't expect to see you here.'

'Why not? It's where you live, isn't it?'

'Yeah, it's where I live.' Her eyes skim over the tall, jungly plants, the beanbags and floor cushions. I know that even though I barely notice it any more, Cat will be smelling the damp, clocking the peeling wallpaper.

'I found you easily,' she's saying. 'I remembered you said the ninth floor, Nightingale House, and I followed the trail of graffiti through the estate . . . is that spray-painted phoenix on that funny little hut down there yours too? This place is cool. I almost got chatted up by two lads who talked like Ali G –'

'It's not cool,' I snap, surprised at the anger in my voice. 'It's a dump!'

'OK,' Cat says, carefully. 'I just thought . . .'

I shake my head. 'No, Cat, you didn't think,' I tell her. 'You just came wandering through the place like some rich-kid tourist on a package tour to trouble. You came to see how the other half live and you think it's cool and edgy and real, but you don't have to live it! You don't know what it's like. It's not a game – it's not an adventure.'

Her face flushes. At my feet, Lucky whines, looking from Cat to me, baffled, and instantly I feel small and mean and spiteful.

I sigh. 'Look, Cat, forget it. It's not your fault. You were always going to say the wrong thing – there is no right thing to say about a place like this.'

She looks at me from under her lashes. 'Different planets, yeah?' she says. 'I might not understand much about your world, but I come in peace!'

I laugh, and the tension falls away. 'It doesn't have to matter, does it?' I say. 'We can still be friends.'

Cat laughs. 'Friends? Boy, you know how to make a girl feel good.'

I'm smiling then, because maybe I didn't want Cat to see me here, but she's here anyhow. She's here because she likes me, and eat your heart out, Neela Rehman, because I know that this time around the attraction isn't Mars bars. Cat likes *me*.

'Well, show me the view then!' she's saying. 'I bet you can see the whole of London, up here!'

I open the glass door that leads out on to the balcony and we pick our way through the growbags stuffed with lettuce, leeks and flowers, the pots overflowing with herbs and climbers, the fruit bushes, the wilting tomato plants still laden with fruit in a home-made polythene greenhouse. One climber twines all around the doorway, dripping with tiny, starry white flowers, and Cat picks a bloom and sticks it behind her ear.

'Wow. You've got more stuff on this tiny balcony than we have in the whole of our back garden!'

'Mum loves it,' I say with a shrug. 'She'd love a proper garden, one day.'

We lean on the balcony rail, looking out over the courtyard below. The Phoenix is just an angled brown roof from here, its garden a blur of paintbox colours. Opposite, the towering outline of Skylark Rise rises up, with Eagle Heights behind it, blocking out the sun as well as anything you could call a view over London.

'The only good view is looking up,' I say, and we tilt our faces up to the blue sky, where a couple of wispy clouds scud along in the breeze.

'No wonder it's called Nightingale House,' Cat says. 'It makes you feel like you can fly!' I look at her face, lit up with wonder, and I want to hug her. She likes it here – she really, really does.

'I bet, when it's dark, you feel like you're close enough to reach out and pick a star right out of the sky!' she breathes.

I don't like to spoil the dream, but I can't help myself. 'There are no stars,' I tell her.

Cat frowns. 'How d'you mean, no stars?'

I look at Cat, and I wonder if she'd understand. I'd like her to, I really would. I lean back against the doorframe, and another piece of my history slips out of its box, out of my mouth. 'There used to be stars, when I was a kid,' I say. 'In the country, when I was staying with my dad. I knew how to pick out the Pole Star – I thought it was my own personal lucky star. Then Dad dumped me and I moved to London. There are too many street lights, too much orange glow – the sky never gets properly dark here. No stars.'

'They're still there, though,' Cat says. 'My dad likes astronomy. He has a telescope in the attic, and he watches the stars on clear nights. He knows all the constellations. The stars are always there, even if you can't always see them.'

I think about what it would be like to have a dad – any dad, let alone one with a hotline to the stars. I think of Cat's dad, imagining an old guy in a cardigan who looks at the night sky and sees past the street light glow, right up to the skies. A dad would look after you, fix things when they broke, earn money for treats and holidays, buy you a bike for Christmas or a puppy of your own. Most dads, anyhow.

Not mine. All I have left of him is a memory of a man who can juggle with fire, a man who thought it was OK to ditch his son to go and live on the other side of the world.

'I don't believe in all that stuff any more,' I answer. 'My luck ran out.'

10

We sit on the beanbags drinking lemonade beneath the big jungly plants.

'Where's your mum then?' Cat wants to know. 'At work? Did you tell her about me?'

'A bit,' I admit.

'What did you say? That I'm gorgeous and clever and funny and brave? That you're mad about me?'

'That you squashed my dog,' I tell her.

'That's just so typical,' she huffs. 'You have to pick out my bad points. She'd like me, I know she would. Shall I hang around until she's home?'

'No, no, Mum won't be back till gone six, and this place is bad news after dark,' I tell her. I try not to look shifty – the truth is, I don't want Cat to meet Mum. Her own mum is pretty, polished, brisk, businesslike. My mum is not.

'Will I meet her another time?' Cat wants to know, but I just shrug.

'She likes all this hippy-dippy stuff, huh?' Cat

persists, looking at the Indian floor cushions, the batik wallhanging, the magazine picture of Buddha peeking out from behind the Swiss cheese plant.

'Too right. She used to be a traveller – a hippy, I suppose,' I explain. 'Years ago.'

'What made her settle down?' Cat asks.

Inside my head, I can feel the memories shifting about inside their little boxes. I need to keep the lids on tight, but with Cat looking at me so intently, it's not easy.

'Just life,' I tell her. 'She got ill and broke up with my dad, and things went a bit wrong for us – we're OK now, though. We've been here almost six years – Mum always says it might be a dump if you look down at the ground, but keep your face to the sun and it's all about blue skies and freedom.'

'She sounds cool,' Cat says, and I just smile.

'So, what's the story with that funny little building down there, the one with the red bird graffiti?' Cat asks. 'It doesn't look like it belongs – all that colour, and the garden. Like your mum's balcony.'

How do you explain a place like the Phoenix Drop-In to a girl like Cat? 'It's just a place,' I tell her. 'Nothing special.'

'But . . .'

Right about then, Lucky jumps up and runs out on to the balcony, barking. 'Good guard dog,' Cat says, and we follow him out.

'Crazy dog, more like,' I say. 'There's nothing there, Lucky, OK? All quiet and peaceful. Seriously, most of the time, nothing ever happens here.'

I trail off into silence as a couple of police cars come screeching into the courtyard below, sirens blazing. They skid to a halt beside the Phoenix, and a bunch of policemen leap out, shove through the gate and into the building.

'Nothing ever happens here, huh?'

I don't even bother to answer. All I can think of is Mum – and Scully. *I can handle him*, she said. I suddenly feel sick, like I know something bad has happened. I'm swearing under my breath, pulling on a hoodie, dragging open the door. Lucky runs out into the corridor, still barking.

'Mouse?' Cat is saying. 'Mouse, what's up? Where are you going?'

My mouth is dry. 'You have to go now,' I tell her. 'I'm sorry, but you really do.' I hold the door wide and she wheels her bike out, wide-eyed. The three of us run along the corridor to the lifts.

'What is it? What's happening? What's wrong?'

The lift doors trundle shut and I feel that awful sensation of falling, like everything safe and stable and reliable is crumbling beneath my feet. 'Mouse?' she says again.

'It's my mum,' I say in a low, angry voice. 'She works at that stupid place, OK? And it turns out

Lucky belongs to one of the local dealers, a real headcase called Scully. He's been hanging round the Phoenix lately. Mum was going to tell him we had Lucky . . .'

I can't look at Cat. If I do, she'll see the fear in my eyes.

The lift crashes to a halt and we run out, across the courtyard to the Phoenix. Cat props her bike against the fence and snaps on the lock. 'You shouldn't even be here,' I say, but Cat just tells me to shut up because she is here, too bad, and I must be crazy if I think she's leaving me now.

Suddenly, the doors swing open and two policeman appear, dragging Scully along in cuffs. He sees Lucky, who is hiding behind my legs, shivering, and his cold eyes lock on to mine, face twisting into a weaselly sneer. 'You skanky little thief . . .'

Suddenly he lunges forward and spits at me. A dribble of slime lands on my hoodie. The police retaliate at once, yanking him away, shoving him into the back of the police car.

'Gross,' Cat whispers. She finds a tissue, wipes away the slime. 'You OK, Mouse?' I nod, but I'm shaking, my face tight with anger. The police car roars away.

I pull Cat into the building. It's a bright, open room that looks like a small herd of elephants just passed through it, turning tables and chairs upside down and splattering the walls with something that looks like spaghetti. Maybe two dozen people are inside, some huddled in groups, shell-shocked, some picking up chairs, straightening tables, wiping walls.

'Mum!' I yell. 'Mum!'

She comes running over and folds me into a quick, tight hug. Lucky runs circuits around us, tail whirling. 'It's OK,' she tells me. 'He had a knife, but Luke got it off him and called the police. It's all OK.'

A knife? It doesn't sound OK to me. Mum holds me at arm's-length, smiling, and I notice for the first time the small wrinkles that curve out around her eyes, her mouth. 'I'm fine, really, Mouse.'

'I'm sorry, I'm so sorry,' I say. 'It's all my fault . . .'

Mum's eyes open wide and she shakes her head.

'No, Mouse,' she says. 'This wasn't your fault – it was nothing to do with you, or Lucky. I never got a chance to even mention all that.'

I frown. 'So, what . . ?'

Mum sighs. 'I caught Scully selling drugs,' she tells me heavily. 'To a couple of new clients, Mark and JJ. I asked him to leave, but he pulled a knife on me . . . luckily, Luke managed to get it off him and Julie called the police.'

'Oh. My. God,' Cat breathes, her mouth a perfect circle of amazement.

Mum turns to Cat, dredging up a smile from somewhere. 'You must be Cat. The girl with the bicycle, right? I'm Magi. Look, I just need to finish giving my statement to the police . . .'

She squeezes my arm and turns away again, and Luke, her colleague, a young black guy with trendy horn-rimmed glasses, claps his hands to get everyone's attention. 'OK, folks, the show's over,' he yells. 'We're gonna close for today – business as usual tomorrow. So if you could all just go home?'

Cat looks bewildered.

'That's Luke,' I explain. 'He works here, with Mum. And that lady over there . . .' I point out an older woman with dyed blonde hair. 'That's Julie – the boss, I guess. She started the place off.'

'What kind of place is it?' Cat wants to know. 'I don't get it. What happened?'

So we sit down in a corner and I tell her that the Phoenix, with its brightly painted walls and flower-filled gardens, is a day centre for recovering drug addicts. They come here to hang out, get a hot meal, get counselling, or just talk, read, play chess, help out in the garden. I watch Cat shift uneasily in her seat as she looks around her, trying to sort out the staff from the clients.

'And that creep who spat at you?' she asks. 'Scully?'

'He's a dealer,' I explain. 'A real lowlife. He's been hanging around, making out he wanted to ditch the drugs, when all the time . . .'

'He was preying on those poor people,' Cat breathes. 'You're telling me he's Lucky's real owner? No way.'

'Way,' I tell her. 'And now he knows we've got Lucky. Trust me, that's very bad news.'

Mum walks over, flanked by a policeman and woman. 'Thanks for calling us,' the policeman is saying. 'Let's hope Mark and JJ are prepared to give evidence in court.'

It's a big 'if', but hope jumps inside me. If Scully goes to prison, he can't come after Mum or hassle the Phoenix clients – and maybe we can keep Lucky? Things might just work out after all.

'This is a great project, but you've had your share of trouble,' the policeman continues. 'Maybe Eden isn't the right place for it?'

Mum puts her hands on her hips. 'It's the best place in the world for it,' she says fiercely. 'This is where it's needed most. You know what the rates of drug abuse are. How many known drug dealers do we have here?'

The policeman looks embarrassed. 'We'd love to clean up the estate,' he says. 'But you know yourself, Magi, people around here just don't care.'

'You're wrong,' Mum argues. 'We do. Look, I'm prepared to stand up and be counted, OK? I'll testify against Scully. I saw it all, and I'm not afraid to stand up in court and say so.'

'You sure?' the policeman asks.

Mum's grey eyes are serious, steady. 'I'm sure,' she says.

When I was eight years old, the social services sent me to see a counsellor. I'd been having bad dreams – seriously, the kind where you shout out in your sleep and yell and fight and wake up covered in sweat. Not good. The counsellor spent a whole year trying to get me to talk things through. 'You have to trust me,' she said. 'I want to help. Anything you say to me will stay private, between us two, but it will help me to help you stop the nightmares. Trust me.'

Yeah, right. Why would I trust her? I didn't trust anybody else in my life back then. Adults let you down, told you lies and left you stranded. That's what I thought. That's what I still think, mostly. They pretend that they're trying to help you, but really they just want you to stay quiet, keep out of trouble, out of sight. It makes their lives easier.

Not Mum, of course. She's different. She loves me, she cares, and if she wasn't always around for me back then, well, that wasn't her choice. She was ill and she couldn't be the perfect mum, but still, she tried.

Anyhow, the counsellor tried everything she could think of to get me to open up. She tried role play, she tried hypnosis, she got me looking at funny little ink-spot pictures and asked me what they reminded me of. 'Ink spots,' I said.

In the end, a whole year on, she pretty much gave up on me. See what I mean about adults? That's what they do. She told me that she couldn't help me to deal with the past if I wouldn't talk to her about it, but that there was still one trick we could use to stop the nightmares.

We? I was the one waking up screaming, wasn't I?

The counsellor's idea was that I take my bad memories one by one and fold them up like so much dirty washing. I had to pack each one in its own little box, a box with a tight lid that I could jam on nice and hard. If I wanted to be extra sure, I could tie a bit of rope round each box, or add a padlock, whatever. Then I had to carry the boxes, one by one, to the furthest corner of my mind, a place I'd never normally go to, and leave them there. It wouldn't matter if the boxes got dusty, or covered in cobwebs, because I would never need the stuff inside them again.

I looked at her like she was crazy. There were

no heaps of dirty washing, no boxes, no rope, no padlocks. 'It's make-believe,' she told me. 'Like a game, in your mind. You want the nightmares to go away, don't you?' I said that I did. 'Then try it, Mouse. Please?'

I tried. I packed each sad, bad memory up and put the lid on tight, and carried the boxes to the furthest corner of my mind, and what d'you know? The nightmares stopped. As long as I kept the past boxed up, it left me alone.

Until now.

I am seven years old. It's three weeks since my dad left for India with his girlfriend, Storm. I'm staying with a woman called Tess and her family, in the Lake District. Tess is a friend of Storm, but she's OK.

Today is Finn's birthday – Finn, Tess's son, my idea of a cool, kind elder brother. I have a sister too here – not a real sister, but real enough. Dizzy, Storm's daughter. She's been dumped here too. She knows how I feel, what it's like to wait for a phone call, a letter, a postcard that never comes.

We're having a bonfire for Finn's birthday. I want to do something special for him, something cool, but when I mention juggling with fire, the way Dad does, they shake their heads. Fire is dangerous, they tell me. I'm not scared of fire, but still, I promise. Instead of the juggling, I practise riding Finn's BMX. I set up the ramps until I can swoop down the hill, hammer up the ramps and fly into the air, right over the top of the bonfire they're building for later. I can do it so well that I build in a wheelspin too.

That night, as the fire is blazing, I stick sparklers all round the back-wheel rim of the BMX and light them quickly. I pedal down the hill, up the ramp and into the air above the blazing bonfire before anyone even knows what I'm doing. 'Look at me!' I yell.

It's a perfect jump, but as I spin the front wheel I feel the pull of a branch in the spokes, and the BMX falters. The back wheel falls towards the flames, and I twist my body sideways, shoving the handlebars away from me, leaping away from the blaze.

And then it's too late, because my throat is full of soft, hot smoke and the flames are all around me, cloaking me in gold, licking and sizzling and burning, burning, burning.

Somebody's screaming, and I sit bolt upright, drenched in sweat and shivering. My breath is coming in great, gasping gulps, and I know that the voice echoing through my head is my own. Lucky is whining and nuzzling my neck, and Mum rushes in, bleary-eyed, her hair sticking up in clumps. 'Mouse, love,' she whispers, putting her arms round me. 'It's OK. Just a dream.'

We sit for a while in the darkness, until I stop shivering and my breathing slows. Mum keeps an arm round my shoulder, strokes my hand, and Lucky presses his worried face against mine, and slowly I come back to the present.

I'm here, on the Eden Estate, in a small, scruffy bedroom with my mum and my dog, and the past is over and done with, long gone. 'It seemed so real,' I whisper. 'I could feel the flames, smell the smoke . . .'

Mum sniffs and frowns, and I realize that I can still smell the smoke. I jump out of bed in my T-shirt and pyjama trousers and together we run through the darkened flat. Mum drags open the front door, looks out along the corridor, but everything is quiet. Then we notice Lucky, standing at the balcony door, scratching at the woodwork, whining, scrabbling.

'No way . . .' Mum whispers.

But you don't stand up to the dealers on the Eden Estate, not even creeps like Scully. You don't upset them. Turn one of them in, even if he deserved it, and you'll be punished – big time. The dealers are getting their revenge for what happened to Scully.

The night is filled with the smell of petrol and

a dark, choking smoke that sticks to your lungs, clogs up your nostrils. And down in the courtyard the Phoenix is more than a smudge of colour in the darkness, it's a whole blaze of bright, burning flames, dancing, roaring, flying up in the air like tiny firebirds.

Mum leans on the balcony rail, tears streaming down her face, and Lucky leans against her, whining softly. In the distance I can hear sirens, but they stay far-off and distant, like a broken promise, as we watch the Phoenix burn.

You can shower off the stink of smoke, but anger's not so easy to wash away. Dealers torched the Phoenix last night, because Mum, Luke and Julie dared to call the police instead of letting Scully and his mates walk all over them. They should have known better than to fight back, and now they're being punished for it – along with everyone who needs the Phoenix.

We smelt the petrol on the air, saw shadowy figures running through the darkness below, but the dealers are smart. By the time the police get round to interviewing them, they'll have alibis, witnesses ready to swear they were nowhere near here last night. The locals won't speak out against them – they wouldn't dare. Drug dealers run the Eden Estate, everyone knows that. You cannot fight them, no matter how angry you may feel, because they're bigger, stronger, angrier than you.

I pour myself a bowl of cornflakes, open a can of dog food for Lucky, but I can't shake the sad, heavy feeling that invades my blood like a poison.

Mum is talking to Julie in the living room, their conversation going round and round in circles. They want to get the Phoenix up and running again, but although the place was insured, it seems that there'll be enquiries. It could be months before there's a payout. 'We don't have months, Magi!' Julie is saying. 'Our clients need us. If we go under, so do they!'

'We won't go under,' Mum says quietly. 'We'll fight back.'

I just about choke on my cornflakes. 'Mum!' I chip in, alarmed. 'Don't do anything stupid, OK?'

'Is it stupid to speak out?' she asks. 'Is it stupid to say something is wrong? Besides, there are other ways to fight back.'

'What ways?'

'Quiet ways,' she tells me.

I listen to Mum and Julie, and slowly I come up with some quiet ways of my own.

Outside, the air is still heavy with smoke and defeat. The Phoenix is a mess of charred beams, a thick, dark soup of stinking ash and embers. The fruit trees that lined the fence have shrunk to bony black skeletons, the flowers and vegetables frazzled to nothing. The chain-link fence survives, collapsed and curled and melted, clinging to the blackened stubs of fence posts. I can't stand to look at it.

Lucky trots ahead, on a lead made from plastic washing line, his nose twitching. We walk past Skylark Rise, round to the back of Eagle Heights where Jake's workshop is, and when I see that the rickety doors are open, I cross over and go inside.

Jake is at the back of the workshop, fitting tinted glass windows to the now black four-wheel drive. 'All right, Mouse?' he says. 'If you're looking for Fitz, he hasn't been in today.'

'OK,' I tell him. 'I wasn't looking for Fitz especially – just had to get out of the flat, y'know?'

'Yeah, I can imagine,' Jake says. 'Bad business, about the Phoenix. Your mum OK?' Jake has a soft spot for Mum.

'She's not great,' I say.

'Suppose not.' Jake sighs, stepping back to survey one shiny black-tinted window. 'Make us a couple of coffees, will you?'

I click on the kettle, spoon Nescafé, sugar and powdered milk into mugs. Jake takes a long look at Lucky, who is sniffing his way around the edges of the workshop, tail twitching happily. 'You kept hold of the dog then,' he says. 'Lucky for you

Frank's off the scene for a while. It's not a good idea to go against people like that, Mouse. They make their own rules, you know that.'

'Like burning down the Phoenix?'

Jake sips his coffee. 'That wasn't Scully,' he says. 'Obviously.'

'Obviously,' I agree. 'It was his mates.'

'Be careful what you're saying,' Jake tells me. 'It could have been an accident. There's no proof, no evidence –'

'C'mon, Jake, you know it was deliberate,' I say. 'Everyone knows. It was a revenge attack, because Mum, Luke and Julie dared to call the police on Scully. What were they meant to do, let the creep push drugs on those ex-addicts, right under their noses?'

'I'm not saying it's right, I'm just saying it's the way things work around here,' Jake says. 'You don't rock the boat.'

'What if you do?'

Jake chucks an arm round my shoulder, and for a moment I feel safe, protected, like nothing too bad could happen.

'You know the score, Mouse,' he says. 'It may not be fair, but it's the way things are on the Eden Estate. Let it go, OK? You don't want to go stirring up a load more trouble, do you? Keep your mouth shut. Keep out of trouble.'

'Is that what you do?' I ask.

'It's what I have to do.'

I work all afternoon, helping Jake to fit the tinted windows in the posh four-wheel drive, peeling off masking tape, vacuuming the inside. I try not to think about the 'businessmen' who own the car, or why they want the colour and the windows and the plates changed. I guess I just don't want to know. Jake gives me a tenner and a bagful of half-used spray cans, and I help him lock up. 'Thanks, Jake,' I say.

'Just remember,' he says as I whistle for Lucky. 'Remember what I said.'

'I'll remember.'

I'll keep my mouth shut, keep out of trouble. The problem is, trouble has a way of finding me.

Next day, I walk Lucky right off the estate and along the quiet, tree-lined streets that lead to Cat's house. I want to breathe air that doesn't smell of smoke, walk pavements that are littered with fallen leaves, not rusting Coke cans and broken glass. In these streets, people don't burn things down just because you do something they don't like.

I walk along Cat's road, looking at the shiny paintwork, the bay windows glinting in the sun. I could be any boy, any place, walking his dog. A man is clipping his privet hedge with electric clippers, so neatly you could balance a mug of tea on top and not spill a single bit.

'Morning,' he says as I pass.

By the time Lucky and I have walked up and down four times, the hedge-clipping man is giving us dodgy looks like we might be axe-murderers or hedge vandals. I hesitate by Cat's gate, unsure.

Maybe her mum is at home. She wasn't too impressed with me last time, and now she probably knows I live on the Eden Estate, where drugs and violence and trouble are normal, the way hedge-clipping is around here. To get past her, I'd need to turn up with a bunch of flowers and a character reference from my head teacher that says I am a nice, respectable boy with good spelling, great prospects and absolutely no tendencies to spray-paint walls in the middle of the night.

An upstairs window creaks open, and Cat leans out.

'You coming in then?' she wants to know. 'Gonna stand there all day?'

'I'm in a hurry,' I shout back. 'Just passing by, can't stop.'

'Whatever,' she says, raising one perfect eyebrow. 'You've been "just passing by" four times in the past ten minutes!'

'These streets all look the same,' I huff.

'Yeah, right. Hang on, I'm coming down . . .'

I sit on the doorstep with Lucky. His tail beats back and forth through the air like a windscreen wiper. Cat grins, opening the door wide. She looks amazing, in a stripy sweater-dress and big black boots, her hair in a bandana. 'Yup. You're in a real hurry, I can see that,' she says.

'Well,' I say carelessly. 'I mean, I didn't call specially, or anything.'

'Sure you didn't.'

We sit together on the squashy settee, sipping Cokes while Lucky slides his nose into the top of the cream enamel swing-bin and snaffles a bit of cheese rind. French stuff, I bet. He'll be digging out the olives next.

'I heard about the fire,' she says. 'I'm really sorry.'

Last night's paper lies on the kitchen table. *Phoenix in Flames*, the headline blares. I lean over, slowly reading the rest.

Police and fire services were called out at three this morning when a day centre for recovering drug addicts caught fire on the notorious Eden Estate. The Phoenix, yesterday the scene of a dramatic arrest, burnt to the ground before fire services reached the scene. Streets leading into the estate had been blocked with torched and stolen cars, in what may have been a deliberate attempt to prolong the blaze.

Petrol cans found near the scene suggest that the blaze was arson. Although nobody was hurt in the fire, locals feel it is unlikely that the Phoenix can rise from the ashes this time.

'I couldn't believe it,' Cat is saying. 'I wanted to see you, speak to you, but Mum and Dad were practically standing guard . . .'

'The estate's not such a great place to be right now. You're better off staying away.'

'Is that what you want?' Cat asks.

'It's not what I want,' I say, frowning. 'It's probably what you should do, though. I'm just telling you.'

'I don't like being told what to do,' Cat says. 'By anybody.'

We sip our Cokes in silence.

'Who'd do that, anyway?' Cat wants to know. 'Burn down a place that's trying to help people?'

I laugh. 'Drug dealers run the whole estate, Cat – Scully's mates. We're not meant to fight back.'

'D'you think the police will find them?'

'Probably not,' I admit. 'No proof. Nobody's gonna grass up the dealers – they're too scared.'

'That's terrible!'

I shrug. 'Tell me about it.' My eyes flicker up to the framed photo on the far wall, some old wrinkly black guy with smiley eyes and a dodgy print shirt. 'That your grandad?'

'It's Nelson Mandela,' Cat says, rolling her eyes.

'Yeah?' The name sounds familiar. I think there's a community centre named after him, maybe, or a primary school.

'He's only one of the greatest freedom fighters that ever lived!' Cat exclaims. 'He stood up for the black people of South Africa, fought so everybody there could be treated as equal. He had courage and determination. He's a hero!'

'OK. What happened to him?'

'He ended up being President of South Africa!'

I frown, and my brain struggles to remember. 'He's not the guy who got stuck in a prison way out on some island for twenty-seven years, is he?'

Cat looks shifty. 'I never said that being a hero was easy. I expect old Nelson thought it was worth it in the end.'

'You don't get many heroes on the Eden Estate,' I tell her.

'There must be something we can do to get people fighting back,' Cat insists.

'You sound just like Mum – she's got all these ideas for getting the Phoenix back in business, for fighting back in a quiet way . . .'

'Well,' Cat says. 'At least she's doing something!'

'Oh, I'm doing something too.'

Cat's lips twitch into a grin. 'Yeah? What's that then? A graffiti protest?'

I shrug. 'It's what I do best, isn't it? As Mum says, there's more than one way to fight back, and sometimes the quiet ways are the most effective. I've got it all planned out.'

Cat snakes an arm along the back of the settee,

and I feel her fingertips moving softly over the nape of my neck. Suddenly every nerve ending in my body is tingling, and my breathing seems kind of shallow, as if I'm holding my breath.

'D'you ever take someone with you, when you go out tagging?' she asks.

'Not . . . not usually,' I say. 'It's easier on your own. Faster, safer.'

'Maybe,' Cat says. 'Wouldn't it help if you had someone to keep a lookout, though? Watch your back?'

'Your mum's not exactly crazy about me,' I say. 'I don't reckon she'll let you sneak out at three in the morning to go to the Eden Estate.'

'But if I could?' Cat pushes. 'If I could get away, would you take me?'

No, my head tells me. Cat is trouble, and trouble is something I have more than enough of already. It's the last thing you need on a graffiti hit, especially on the estate. Looking out for yourself is hard enough – I don't need the hassle of looking out for someone else.

'Maybe,' I hear myself say. 'You any good at spelling?'

'Brilliant,' Cat tells me. 'Top of the class.'

That figures. 'Well, my spelling's not so good,' I tell her. 'Maybe you could help out. Wear a hat, gloves, scarf, dark clothes. And running shoes.'

I get up abruptly, walk across the kitchen, away from those soft, smooth fingertips on the nape of my neck, making my senses go crazy.

'OK,' Cat breathes, her eyes all lit up. 'I'll be there. I'll say I'm sleeping over at a mate's – someone nice and respectable. No problem.'

'It's not a game, Cat,' I say, and I'm not just talking about the graffiti.

She laughs, green eyes dancing. Lucky has jumped up on to the settee beside her, and her long tawny fingers are stroking his fur now. 'Oh, Mouse,' she says. 'Of course it's a game. Don't you know that? Everything is.'

Cat stands on the doorstep of the little, ivy-covered house and waves as her mum drives away. She chats for a minute to a pretty Asian girl, then her friend closes the door gently and Cat turns back towards the street. Lucky and I slip out from the shadows and Cat just about jumps out of her skin.

'What took you so long?' I grin.

We fall into step together. 'OK?' I ask. 'Your parents weren't suspicious? Your friend won't grass you up?'

'Aditi's cool,' she says. 'She won't tell. Relax.'

We walk through the darkening streets and into the Eden Estate. Cat slips her hand into mine as gangs of kids on bikes whirl round and round in the dark. A dozen lads have made skateboard ramps from old wooden boards propped up on breeze blocks. They rattle up and down, making clunking turns and swooping ollies, lit up by the blazing headlights of a clapped-out car parked squint in the road, pumping out skate rock at full volume.

'Mouse, man, you gonna introduce your girlfriend?' Fitz yells from the edge of the group. 'Or are you scared of the competition?'

'When you get fed up with him, give me a call,' Chan adds.

'Not gonna happen,' Cat shouts back, laughing. Fitz and Chan grin, going back to their ramps. They are impressed with Cat. Who wouldn't be?

We head on, past Eagle Heights and Skylark Rise. Psycho Sam, a big bloke from the first floor on Nightingale House, walks past with his two Rottweilers, scowling. He's had a grudge against Fitz, Chan and me since we broke a window with a badly aimed football, back when we were eight. Cat laughs when I tell her the story.

We come to a halt where the Phoenix used to be.

'Whoa,' Cat whispers, taking in the charred wreckage. Then her eyes pick out a clump of jewel-red flowers poking up through the ashes, green stems bright against the dusty grey. Further back there's another clump, and another. 'The flowers!' she gasps. 'I don't get it – how did they survive when everything else . . . ?'

'They didn't,' I tell her. 'Mum planted them, this morning. It's a protest, to show she's not giving up on the place. That there's still hope.' We turn away,

97

towards Nightingale House with its lobby littered with broken glass and cigarette stubs.

'Does she know what you're planning?' Cat asks.

'We haven't talked about it,' I reply. 'She knows I'm going to do something, though. She won't try to stop me.'

We scuff our way into the lift, press the button for the ninth floor. Someone has dropped a takeaway carton in the corner, an oily puddle of chicken tikka masala. 'She's OK with me staying over?' Cat presses.

'As long as your parents are fine with it,' I shrug. 'So you can maybe avoid mentioning the fact that they haven't a clue you're here. Yeah?'

'Sure,' Cat says. 'It's cool your mum's planted those flowers . . . it's like new life coming out of the ashes, y'know?'

'I know. She won't let this beat her – nor will Luke and Julie.'

'It's great that they care so much,' Cat says.

We come out of the lift, start walking along to number 114. 'They care more than you'd think,' I say. 'Julie started the Phoenix, six years ago when her daughter died of an overdose. Luke lost his little brother the same way.'

The colour drains from Cat's face. 'Scary,' she says, with a shudder.

'Too right,' I hear myself say. 'I used to lie awake at night, when I was a kid, watching the stars. Even before Dad took off for India, he wasn't exactly looking out for me, but I had this crazy idea that nothing bad could happen if I could just see the stars. I was scared that if I fell asleep then maybe, in the dark, everything would go wrong . . . and I had nightmares, awful nightmares too. I was so sure I'd lose Mum.'

'Magi?' Cat asks, wide-eyed. 'But why would you worry about her?'

I rake a hand through my hair and look at Cat for a long moment. Bit by bit, her wide green eyes are tugging every memory, every fragment of my past from the places they've stayed hidden for so long.

'Because she was a junkie,' I say.

Cat's eyes widen as she takes in the chaotic rainbow that is my bedroom. 'Whoa,' she says. 'It's like being inside the best graffiti picture ever.'

The walls of my room may be crazy, but as your eyes roll up towards the ceiling, there's less chaos, more blue. The ceiling is like a night sky without stars. Cat peers at the threadbare dream catcher hanging above my bed, stroking the feathers. I slide a Fall Out Boy CD into my player, and we flop down on beanbags.

'Tell me,' she says. 'About when you were a kid, watching the stars. About your mum.'

So I tell her the stuff that I never tell anybody, the stuff I don't even let myself think about any more. I thought it was safely packed away, behind closed doors, but the minute I start to speak the memories just keep coming, and Cat listens, silent.

I tell her that Mum got into drugs when my dad left, when I was just two years old. She was pretty cut up about the split, and the drugs were a way of taking the edge off the pain. Pretty soon, of course, the drugs created more pain, more hurt, than the break-up ever had.

'That's what she told me later, anyhow,' I explain. 'As a kid, I just thought it was normal – I suppose I was too young to know better. We lived in squats and scruffy flatshares with other junkies, and Mum did whatever she could to find the money for her next fix. She stole, she begged, she did other things . . .' I trail off into silence. I don't even want to think about it. Cat is looking at me, wide-eyed. I search her face for traces of pity, but find only concern.

'She was still a good mum,' I tell Cat. 'She made sure I had food and clothes and a safe place to stay. I knew I was loved.'

Cat's fingers trace the line of my wrist, the creased skin of my palm. 'It was OK,' I say, softly.

'I mean, of course, it wasn't great, but back then I didn't know any different. When I was seven, everything changed. Mum overdosed – she almost died, and while she was in the hospital recovering, she asked if they could help her get off the drugs. She did it for my sake – she wanted to be there to see me grow up.'

Cat bites her lip.

'I didn't know that at the time, though. I just knew she was ill. I was sent to live with my dad, Zak. He was a hippy – he had a tepee and he travelled around the music festivals with his new girlfriend in an old VW van.'

'He's the one who could juggle with fire,' Cat says, and I remember telling her that, the day she nicked the chocolates in Covent Garden, as we sat watching the street jugglers.

'That's right,' I say. 'He was tall and tanned, with blonde dreadlocks that reached right down his back. I wanted to be just like him, but he didn't even notice I was alive. I was just a nuisance, as far as he was concerned.'

'Oh, Mouse.'

I take a deep breath in. There's too much stuff hidden away in my head. I was crazy to think it would ever stay there. I feel like running through the neatly folded memories, kicking them to pieces, pulling them out into the daylight where everyone can see. Well, not everyone. Just Cat.

'It wasn't so bad,' I tell her. 'Staying with Zak.
I got to run wild every day, out in the countryside.
I got to eat proper meals and I made some friends
– more like family, really. In some ways it was the
best summer I ever had – in other ways, it was
the worst. I got into trouble pretty much the whole
time, but I had fun too. I taught myself to juggle,
I went to the beach, I slept in a tree house. I was
happy, a lot of the time, but still, I worried about
Mum. I couldn't forget the way she'd looked the
day she overdosed . . . so still, so pale. Her lips
were blue. I thought she was going to die, Cat.'

'So you stayed awake at night and watched the
stars.'

'Waste of time,' I say gruffly. 'Everything went
wrong anyway. Dad took off for India and the
whole summer fell apart. I ended up back in
London, in care. I had foster-parents for a year,
this very kind, very serious couple, Jan and Paul.
I got to see Mum every week until she was well
enough to look after me again. Social services found
us a place to live, and we've been here ever since.
It's not much, but it's ours, y'know?'

This is not something I've ever talked about
before, not even with Mum – we've lived through
it once after all. We don't want to go back there.
I'm quiet, remembering the little boy who slept in

a tree house under the stars, wondering if his mum would ever get better or his dad would ever learn to love him.

'Thanks,' Cat whispers. 'For telling me.'

'Thanks for listening,' I say.

For the first time ever, the bad memories don't seem so scary, so dark, as if sharing them has stripped them of their power to hurt me. Cat listens and understands, as if knowing about my past helps her to know me.

Who knows, one day I might even tell her the very worst memory of all.

'I got you a present,' Cat says into the silence, fishing a small, tissue-wrapped parcel out of her bag. 'It was because of what you said the other day, about there being no stars in London. And then I read about the Phoenix and I know it's stupid, but I suppose I wanted you to have something to believe in again . . .'

'A present?'

'I paid for it,' she says, quickly. 'Promise.'

I can't remember the last time anyone bought me a present, when it wasn't my birthday or Christmas or anything. I rip open the wrapping. Inside are three packets of white glow-in-the-dark stars, the kind with a peel-off backing that little kids might stick on to walls and furniture. I start to laugh.

Cat frowns. 'You don't think it's babyish?'

I can't stop laughing, but it's not because I think the present is babyish, it's because it's the best present I've ever had. 'You bought me stars!' I exclaim. 'You actually bought me stars!'

Cat grins. 'Well, there's this little shop, about a hundred million light-years from here . . .'

I hug her quickly, still laughing, and she feels small and light and soft in my arms. Her hair smells of vanilla. I'd like to go on holding her, but that's not a good idea. I know I'd never want to let go.

I step back, tearing open the first packet of stars, peeling off the backing. I jump up on to the rickety chest of drawers to stick them on the ceiling. Cat hands me up some more, and then we drag the chest of drawers all around the room so I can reach every bit of ceiling space.

By the time Mum sticks her head round the door to see what all the racket is, the deep blue ceiling is sprinkled with glow-in-the-dark stars. 'Fantastic!' she breathes. 'It's like your own private galaxy in here, Mouse!'

She switches the light off and the stars blink and shimmer, fading slowly away to nothing, and in the darkness Cat's hand finds mine and holds on, tight.

The first thing I see when I wake is a ceiling full of stars, glinting softly, and my mouth twitches into a smile. I crawl out of bed and dress quickly in old jeans, a hoodie and ancient Converse trainers. My watch reads three minutes past three.

I creep into the living room, Lucky at my heels. Everything is still, silent. Mum's big, leafy plants loom over me as I look down at Cat, curled in her sleeping bag in a pink *Hello Kitty* nightdress, corkscrew curls spread out around her face like a dark halo. I kick her gently with the toe of my trainer while Lucky snuffles her ear.

'Cat! Cat, wake up!'

She groans and stretches in the half-light. 'Ugh, Lucky, don't!' she hisses, struggling to sit upright.

'Bathroom's free,' I whisper. 'Don't take forever.'

She creeps across to the bathroom, emerging soon after dressed in black jeans and jacket. I grin, picking up a rucksack full of spray cans.

'Where d'you get the paint?' Cat whispers.

'My mate's dad has a garage. He lets us wash cars and help out. Mostly, I get paid in spray cans.'

Lucky trails us to the door, glum. 'Not tonight, pal,' I say. 'I want you to look after Mum.'

The lift plummets down from the ninth floor. 'What if we get caught?' Cat wants to know.

'We won't,' I scoff. 'I've never been caught. Not till afterwards, anyhow. And you can act as lookout.'

'Did I tell you I'm shortsighted?' she teases.

'Knew there had to be a reason you were hanging out with me.'

The lift sighs to a halt and we walk out across the lobby and into the cold night air. The estate is deserted except for a bow-legged Staffie sniffing around near Nightingale House. Distant reggae beats drift down from a far-off balcony.

'Any CCTV to watch out for?' Cat asks. 'Security cameras and stuff?'

'Sometimes,' I tell her. 'Not now. They smashed them all up before the fire on Monday night. Just stay away from the street lights.'

I've planned it all out in my head, and the first hit is Skylark Rise, a big grey expanse of wall just left of the entrance lobby. I set my bag down, pull my hood up and take out a can of paint. 'OK?' I ask Cat, and she grins back, nodding, watching.

I take a deep breath and begin, spraying the

outline of a phoenix, then filling in the detail of the outstretched wings with crimson and purple. I work quickly, confidently, switching to yellow, red and orange to paint a line of curling flames beneath the phoenix. I look over my shoulder at Cat. 'OK,' I grin. 'My spelling's hopeless, and I don't want any mistakes on this. Spell *phoenix* for me, yeah? Slowly! Then *rising*, OK?'

She spells the words, letter by letter, and the legend *phoenix rising* appears, in a perfect curve above the red bird. 'It's cool,' Cat breathes. 'Whoa!' I chuck my paint can into the bag and we move off, just as a police car swoops in from the main road and makes a slow circuit of the estate.

'Omigod!' Cat yelps. 'They'll see it! They'll know it was us!'

'Keep walking,' I tell her. 'Head down. They won't even notice the graffiti, and if they do, they won't care. The police have more important things to worry about around here, y'know?'

'What if they stop us? Search your bag?'

But the police car has gone, and I'm laughing. 'Nervous, huh?' I ask. 'Don't worry. Just keep your ears open, as well as your eyes.'

I paint a second giant phoenix on to the wall of Eagle Heights, then target smaller areas. I spray a colourful *dealers out* on a bit of low wall beside the kids' playground, again on a row of boarded-up windows and a third time on the corrugated metal shutters of the estate's single shop. *No to drugs* is the last slogan, sprayed in letters three feet high on the wall round the bins at the back of Skylark Rise and all along the lock-up garages that edge the back of the estate.

We share a Mars bar, huddled side by side on the wall beside the garages. It's past five now, and the sky is beginning to lighten, but I want to paint one last phoenix. I pick out a huge, scabby wall at the side of a block called Raven's Crest, start blocking in the shape and adding detail to the wings and tail. I'm buzzing. I use up the last of the yellow and orange paint on flames that swirl up to frame the phoenix, and Cat does her dictionary bit, spelling the words out as I spray *phoenix rising* above the artwork.

'Done,' I whisper. 'What d'you think?'

'I think you're crazy,' Cat tells me. 'You're really talented, you know? And these are going to cause one big stir tomorrow, but . . . well, don't you ever get scared?'

'Scared?' I echo. 'No way! It's the best feeling in the world!'

Right then, a middle-aged couple turn the corner by the flats, walking right towards us. I kick the rucksack of paint into the shadows, turn away, but Cat has a better idea. She slides her arms round me, pulling me back against the wall. 'Shhh,' she whispers, burying her face against my shoulder.

I shut my eyes against the soft, springy ringlets of her hair, listening to the tip-tap of high-heeled boots and the low murmur of voices as the couple pass by. I can hardly breathe, but I don't think it's anything to do with fear.

'They've gone,' I whisper. Cat lifts her head, and her cheek brushes mine. Neither of us makes any move to pull apart. 'Cat?' I whisper again.

Then my fingers slide up into her hair and my mouth finds hers, and we're kissing. Her lips are soft and warm and she tastes faintly of Mars bar, which is not a bad way for a girl to taste, I promise you. After a little while, I break away.

'We should get back,' I whisper.

'We should.'

Then I'm kissing her again, and I can feel the soft, vanilla-scented touch of her hair against my cheek and my insides feel all warm and gooey. I want that feeling to last forever. It doesn't, of course. A police siren starts up somewhere nearby, and we pull apart as headlights rake through the darkness. 'That's all we need . . . time to go!'

I pick up the rucksack and grab Cat's hand and we're out of there, running as fast as we can, laughing, breathless, into the night.

16

Back at the flat, we sit on beanbags under the big leafy plants, sipping hot chocolate. Lucky is curled up between us, me scratching his tummy, Cat tickling his ears.

'My lookout skills weren't so good towards the end there,' Cat says. 'Sorry about that. Disappointed?'

'No way,' I laugh. 'With you? No way.'

She grins in the half-light. 'Well, I guess that's because you just don't know me very well,' she says, but she's grinning all the same. 'I'm not as perfect as you think.'

'No,' I agree. 'Your spelling's OK, though.'

She chucks a cushion at me and I catch it before it hits the Swiss cheese plant, laughing. 'Who cares about perfect?' I ask. 'I like you anyhow. You gave me stars.'

'I wish I could give you the real kind,' she says.

'You did,' I tell her.

'My dad told me once that every last one of us on this earth is made from stardust,' Cat says softly.

My heart jumps. 'What?' I ask. 'Made of stardust? No way.'

'There's a big scientific explanation for it, obviously,' Cat says. 'My dad likes astronomy and looking at the stars, so he knows all kinds of stuff about them. That's what it comes down to, though. We're made from stars. I like the idea of that.'

'I do too,' I say. 'Your dad sounds cool.'

'He's OK,' Cat says, uncertainly. 'I suppose. He works too hard. He never has time for me.'

I hold up my hand in the darkened room, spread the fingers wide. Skin, bone, blood . . . or stardust? How could there not be magic and hope and miracles in the world, if all of us were made of stars? Cat must have it wrong. There's no magic around here, that's for sure.

But when she catches my hand in the darkness, holding it tight, I'm not so sure. 'Do you ever wish you could go back in time?' she asks me. 'Turn the clock back to when things really were perfect? When you were a kid, y'know, and happy?'

I frown, because the closest I've ever been to perfect is here and now, holding hands with a green-eyed girl who thinks I'm made from stardust. 'The past wasn't such a great place, for me,' I remind her.

'I guess not,' she says. 'Wouldn't you like to go back, though? Do things differently?'

I can tell from the longing in her voice that Cat would, but I also know that there's no going back, no matter what. I shrug. 'Things would still have happened the same way,' I tell her.

'Do you think so?' she asks. 'I'm not so sure. I wouldn't mind trying to make things different.'

She makes a snuffling sound in the dark. 'You OK?' I ask.

'Hay fever,' she says, but I don't think you can get hay fever in October. She's crying. Maybe the past wasn't such a great place for Cat, either.

I find a box of tissues and hand her some, watch as she wipes her eyes. 'Want to talk about it?' I ask.

'Nope,' she says. 'Everyone has their dark secrets, don't they?'

'Maybe,' I say. 'But . . . well, talking about it can help, y'know.'

'Talk then,' Cat says in a muffled voice. 'Tell me about what happened after your dad went away. Did you stay in touch with the people you met, that summer?'

'I tried,' I say. 'When Dad went to India, everything changed. I ended up in London, with the foster-parents I told you about, Jan and Paul. I wasn't much good at letters. I couldn't read or write at all back then – I was learning, at school, but it was tough. I'd get Jan and Paul to write for me, or send pictures I'd drawn maybe. Dad never answered. Not ever.'

Cat bites her lip.

'I got letters back from one friend, for a while,' I go on. 'Dizzy – she was like a big sister to me, even though we weren't related. Her mum was Dad's girlfriend – the one he took off to India with. She rang a few times, and I'd write to her and send her pictures for this other guy, Finn, and biscuits for the dog, Leggit.'

'How come you lost touch?' Cat asks. Her voice seems clearer now, softer, as if getting wrapped up in my past has chased her sadness away.

'It was when I went to live with Mum again,' I say. 'We moved here – I had to change schools and there was nobody to help me with my writing any more. I stopped trying.'

Cat frowns. 'But why couldn't your mum . . ?'

I sigh. 'She can't write, Cat. Not at all.' In the thin dawn light, her face is serious, shocked, struggling to understand. How could she? I bet her mum went to university and everything.

I get up, pad across the scratchy nylon carpet to my bedroom, reappearing with a shoebox and a duvet. I flop down again, wrap the duvet round myself. 'These are the letters,' I tell Cat, taking the lid off the shoebox. 'Four of them. I kept them all.'

'Your friend didn't keep on writing, after you stopped?'

'Maybe,' I shrug. 'If she did, nobody ever passed the letters on. She never had this address, and Jan and Paul – well, they thought all of those people from my past were bad news.'

'Why?'

'They had their reasons. They were wrong about Dizzy and Finn, though.'

'You could get in touch now,' Cat suggests.

'No. I've left it too late – I wouldn't know what to say.'

I reach for the shoebox, lift out a letter from the mess of seashells, friendship bracelets, crystals and festival tickets from long ago. I scan through the childish, curly handwriting. It says that Leggit is going to dog-training classes and Finn sends his love, and have I heard anything yet from India, because Dizzy hasn't, but we're bound to soon, don't worry. Oh, and thanks for the Mars bar.

Across the room, Cat huddles in her sleeping bag. She holds out her hand and I pass the letter over for her to read. Outside, on the balcony, sunrise streaks the sky behind Skylark Rise with shades of pink and peach and purple. I curl up, eyes closed, and fall into sleep.

I wake up to swirling, New Age music and the smell of cooked breakfast. Mum is in the kitchen, singing along to a CD player, clanking pans and sipping coffee. On the other side of the room, Cat groans and burrows down into her sleeping bag, pursued by Lucky.

'Sleep OK?' Mum asks from the open doorway. She doesn't seem to notice that Cat and I went to bed at half ten last night in separate rooms, then woke up fully dressed in the living room. Well, I guess she notices, but just doesn't mind. I clear away the shoebox and the duvet, then wash and pull a comb through my hair. It doesn't make much difference – I still look like I slept in a hedge.

'Breakfast's ready!'

Mum and Cat are tucking into toast, scrambled eggs, baked beans and mushrooms, grinning together. Cat looks bright-eyed and wide awake, like she just spent the night in a five star hotel instead of curled up in a sleeping bag on a nylon carpet. 'This is good,' she says. 'Thanks, Magi!'

'You're welcome,' Mum replies. 'How did it go, anyway? The art project?'

Cat just about chokes on her toast. I shrug. 'OK,' I say. 'You can see for yourself, later.'

'He thinks he's some kind of modern-day Van

Gogh,' Mum tells Cat. 'Only with both ears intact, of course.'

Cat swallows a forkful of scrambled eggs, wide-eyed. This is probably not the kind of conversation she'd have with her mum, a strict but successful lawyer. The first whiff of rebellion and she'd be grounded for the rest of her life. Longer, maybe. Me and Mum have a different kind of relationship, more like friends than mother and son, or maybe just like two people who have come through a lot of bad stuff together and managed to survive.

Later, as I walk Cat back across the estate, Lucky trotting beside us on his washing-line lead, I see Mrs S., Scully's gran. She is on her knees in the ashes where the Phoenix used to be, digging away with a spoon. 'Mrs S., what are you doing?' I ask, dropping down beside her.

Her wrinkled face breaks into a smile. 'Well, I saw what your mother had done, planting those flowers,' she says. 'I thought I'd do the same. I got some lovely winter pansies from the supermarket!'

'Cool,' I tell her. 'You could do with a trowel, though, to plant them.' I take the spoon and scrape away at the ash and soil until a couple of little holes appear, and Mrs S. lifts her plants into place and presses the soil down round them. She takes a plastic bottle of water from her shopping bag and soaks the flowers, then packs the bottle, the spoon and the empty plastic pot away inside her bag. I help her to her feet.

'I'm not the only one, either,' she says, and I look again. Half a dozen new plants are sticking up through the rubble since yesterday. I can't help smiling. In a small way, the locals are fighting back.

'It's a great idea,' Cat tells her. 'Magi's gonna love it!'

'Some of that dreadful graffiti art has sprung up overnight too,' she tells us. 'I don't approve of it, mind, but it shows people are angry about the blaze. Tell your mum that – people care.'

She takes a long look at Lucky, who gives her a winning smile. 'He really does look like my Frankie's dog,' she says. 'But now that I see him in daylight, it's very clear he's yours. That's a good thing, Mouse, what with my Frankie being away for a while. Look after him.'

I swallow. 'I will, Mrs S.,' I tell her. 'Promise.'

Mrs S. turns back towards Nightingale House, then stops and looks back over her shoulder. 'Frankie's not really a bad boy,' she says. 'Tell your mum that, Mouse. He just got in with the wrong people, lost his way.'

'Of course,' I tell her.

I wish I could believe it.

The doorbell rings, and when I open the door there's a girl in a black net tutu and fluffy black fairy wings standing on the doorstep. Her face is painted white, and she has black lipstick and smudged eyeliner, like an emo panda. Her corkscrew curls are piled up on her head, tied with black velvet ribbon, and she's wearing a kid's hairband with a spangly bat at the front.

'Wow!' I say.

The black fairy looks cross. 'You're supposed to scream,' she tells me. 'Or shudder, or faint. You don't just say "wow".'

'Sorry,' I grin. 'You walked across the Eden Estate looking like that?'

'I flew,' she says, tugging at the black fairy wings. 'Look, I haven't got all night. Trick or treat?'

'We don't usually get people coming round,' I apologize. 'No treats. Sorry.'

'Nothing?' she says, crestfallen. 'No sweets, no monkey nuts, no fruit?'

'There's half a tin of beans in the fridge,' I say.

'You're too good to me, Mouse.'

Cat pushes me into the flat, right up against the coatrack. Then she kisses me, and her lips taste of sugar and facepaint. 'Who is it?' Mum calls through from the living room, and we pull apart.

'You did have a treat, after all,' Cat says with a sly grin.

'It's just Cat, Mum,' I shout. 'I'll bring her through!'

'Your lipstick's smudged,' Cat says carelessly, and I glance in the hall mirror just in time to wipe away the smears of black and white imprinted on my mouth.

'Happy Hallowe'en!' she says, giving Mum a couple of penny chews from her black plastic cauldron. 'Can Mouse come trick-or-treating? We won't be late.'

'I suppose,' Mum says. 'Not around the estate, though – it's not safe. And don't be too late . . .'

'We won't,' Cat says, producing a pair of devil horns and a pointy tail from her cauldron. 'I knew you wouldn't be prepared, so I brought these. OK?' I slide the horns on over my fringe and tuck the tail into the back of my drainpipes. 'I didn't forget you,' she tells Lucky, fixing a length of black tinsel round his collar. 'There – perfect!'

'So,' Cat wants to know as we wait for the lift. 'Was it you then? The spray paint?'

'What spray paint?' I ask.

Then the lift arrives, the door wheezes open and I see that someone has painted the whole of the inside a soaring turquoise blue. It's like stepping inside your own, private piece of sky. 'Cool,' I say.

'Not you then,' Cat says. 'I guess someone was fed up with the swear word graffiti and the curry sauce stains. Thought you said people around here just don't care?'

'They don't,' I say. 'Not usually. This is a first.'

Cat raises an eyebrow. 'It's a good sign,' she tells me. 'People are trying to change things.'

We mooch past the Phoenix, where yet more bright flowers and climbers twine amongst the ruins. We get a few shouted insults from the kids down by the playground. Cat just laughs and chucks them a load of penny chews, and they look at us like we're crazy. Outside the estate, things are just as strange. Cat doesn't want to call from house to house, collecting sweets. Instead, she stops gangs of small children dressed up as witches and goblins, handing them sweets and biscuits printed with spiders' webs.

'Why are you giving us sweets?' one small vampire demands.

'I want to,' Cat says. 'It's fun. Tell me a joke or something, OK?'

'Why didn't the skeleton go to the Hallowe'en disco?'

'Dunno,' Cat says.

''Cos he had no body to dance with. D'you get it? No body?'

'Cool,' Cat says, and hands him a jelly snake.

'I think you've got the rules of Hallowe'en a little bit muddled,' I say.

'So what?' Cat grins. 'I like my rules better.'

'I like your rules better too,' I admit, as another small knot of ghouls heads off into the night. 'You're good with kids.'

'I used to be,' Cat says. 'Once. Look, I'm all out of sweets now. We'll go back to mine.'

We turn into her road, Lucky straining at his washing-line lead, trailing tinsel. 'School on Monday,' Cat says. 'Can you believe it? How come we get eight weeks of school for every week of holiday? That doesn't seem right.'

'Kind of unbalanced,' I agree.

'Shall we skive off, go up to town again?'

'Cat, no way,' I tell her. 'You know I have to be on my best behaviour after the exclusion. I promised Mum, and Dodgy Dave.'

'D'you always do what Dave tells you?' she asks.

I laugh. 'Hardly ever,' I admit. 'But he's OK, for a social worker – I don't want to let him down.'

We stop on the pavement outside her gate. 'Let's go in, anyhow,' she says. 'You have to get your treat, I've got it all planned . . .'

'If I see another sweet I think my teeth might melt,' I confess.

'Who said it was sweets? Mum and Dad are out, and it's a cool, clear night . . .'

A cool, clear night? I'm not sure why this matters, unless it means we have to huddle together for warmth or something. The idea of that has me feeling hot all over, then breaking out in a cold sweat.

Cat leads me along the path and into the hallway that still smells of coffee and spices, but this time we don't head for the kitchen. She drags me upstairs. 'Is this a good idea?' I ask, as she steers me along the landing and up a second flight of stairs. 'I can't stay too late . . .'

We're on the second storey now, creeping along a little landing under slanting eaves, past attic rooms. 'Relax!' she tells me. 'We won't be late, anyhow. My parents'll be back at eleven, and you have to be out of here by then or I'm dead meat . . .'

She pushes open a pine door and shoves me into the room, with Lucky at my heels. It's dark inside and Cat doesn't switch on the light, but my eyes adjust and I can see from the light on the landing that this is not a bedroom. It's a study, built into the roof of the house beneath glossy Velux windows that face the sky. Right in the centre of the room is a telescope, a proper telescope, on a stand, like you'd see at a museum or something. It's pointing up at the windows, towards the night sky.

'Oh, man,' I whisper. 'How cool?'

'Thought you'd like it,' she smirks. 'It's Dad's. You can have a look, if you like. On a cool, clear night you can usually see the stars. I wanted to show you that they really are there, even if you can't see them without a telescope.'

I take a step forward, unfasten the lens cap. I blink and swivel the telescope slightly, then gasp as the sky comes into focus. The orange haze has gone, and in its place is a blanket of darkness pierced here and there by tiny, glittering diamonds. Cat was right. Above us is a perfect sky, filled with stars. 'Well?' she wants to know, tugging at my elbow. 'What d'you think? Trick or treat?'

I grin. 'Treat,' I tell her. 'Most definitely, treat.'

Cat brings up mugs of hot chocolate and a slice of French cheese for Lucky, and we sit on the floor looking up at the attic windows, looking past the orange haze to the velvet sky beyond. 'It's like one of those magic-eye pictures,' Cat tells me. 'Once you know what to look for, you can see it.'

'Your dad must know loads about the stars,' I say. 'Is that what he does? Is he a scientist or something?'

'No, no, this is just his hobby,' she says, vaguely. 'He knows lots about it, though. The names of the constellations and all that. He used to show me, when I was younger.'

'Not now?'

Cat shrugs. 'He's too busy, these days.' She gets up and switches on the light, and suddenly the windows to the sky are just two dull rectangles of glass in the slanting ceiling. The telescope looks smaller under the electric light, a spindly thing stranded in the middle of the carpet. The walls are covered with maps and charts, patterns of stars and lines and scribbles.

'What are these?' I ask Cat.

'Star maps,' she tells me. 'They show you how to find the constellations. It's just like with an ordinary map – it shows you where you are in the sky. The one you're looking at is for the constellation of Orion the Hunter – these three stars make up his belt. That's his sword, and that's his shield . . .'

I frown. 'I can't see it,' I admit. 'Looks like someone's been scribbling over a dot-to-dot book without following the numbers.'

'I know . . . but that's what those stars looked like to the first astronomers, thousands of years ago. This shape here is Orion's companion, the Great Dog . . .' Cat points to a chart of dots and lines that looks like a jerky sketch of a lopsided dog.

'Hear that, Lucky?' I grin. 'You've got your own constellation!'

'And a star,' Cat says. 'Sirius – the Dog Star.'

Lucky's tail beats against the carpet, like he knew this all along. I sit down, leaning back against the desk. 'A star map, to help you find your way around the night skies,' I say. 'Wish I'd known that when I was sticking up those stars at home the other day.'

Cat rolls her eyes. 'What, are you gonna peel

them all off again and arrange them like this?' she scoffs, nodding at the charts. 'I didn't have you down as someone who followed the rules, Mouse. Why don't you make your own stories up?'

'I suppose,' I say.

'That's what I do,' Cat says. 'I have my own theories about the sky, my own version of a star map. Ever see that Disney film, *The Lion King*?'

I nod. I remember seeing it on video, not long after I moved in with Jan and Paul. All that stuff about fathers and sons really upset me, coming just after Dad took off for India.

'Remember how the lion king tells Simba he'll always be there with him?' she says. 'In the stars? Well, that's kind of like what I believe too. That people who are special to you are always with you, even when you can't see them any more. Like when someone's dead . . .'

'. . . or gone away,' I finish for her.

Cat is silent for a moment, sniffing a little in the darkness. 'What I'm saying is, they never really leave you,' she says softly. 'They live on inside you, no matter what. You can forget the names those old astronomers gave to the stars, call them whatever you want . . . names that mean something to you.'

'So I could call the Dog Star Lucky, not Sirius,' I say.

'That's right. Each one of us can have our own unique star map, our own constellations and star names. That way, we're never alone.'

She looks so sad, so lost, that for a moment I want to hold her hands and tell her that she'll never be alone, because she has me now. I just don't know if that's enough. Her green eyes are misty, and she wipes a hand across them, impatiently. 'Stupid face paint,' she says, smiling. 'Gets in your eyes.'

'Yeah?'

'Yeah.'

I move up beside her so that my arm can curl right round her, and she turns her head so that her cheek rests against my fringe. 'I wish I could grab you a bunch of real stars, Mouse. I would if I could.'

Then we're kissing, and I feel like I'm floating, way, way up in the night sky, a hunter called Orion with a belt made of stars and a dog at my heels. I could be anywhere, nowhere, and then suddenly I come hurtling back down to earth with a bang. Cat's fingers trace along the line of my jaw, creeping higher.

I grab her wrist and hold her still. 'No,' I whisper.

My heart thuds. I'm not sure that Cat is ready to handle this: my secret, the darkest memory of all.

'What is it with this fringe?' she says, huffily. She

pulls free of my grip and strokes my hair softly, blowing against it with warm, sweet breath. I close my eyes and wait, my heart thumping, and sure enough her fingers push up through my fringe, raking it back from my face. I feel her stop, I feel her freeze, and suddenly my chest is so tight I can barely breathe.

'Oh, Mouse,' she says.

Her fingers touch my cheekbone, my temple, my ear, the stretched, puckered skin that nobody ever sees. She doesn't flinch. It's like the flutter of a bird's wings, a butterfly kiss.

'What happened?' she asks.

I shake my head, but Cat just rests her mouth against the ruined skin and her fingers slide down my face as the hair drops back down to hide the scars. After a while, I can breathe again, and finally I tell her about how it all happened, how that summer ended, long ago when I was seven.

Dad went off to India, leaving me behind with an ache where my heart had been. Was I so unlovable? Finn and Dizzy didn't think so. They believed in me, and in return I idolized them.

The nightmare is still fresh – it always will be. Finn's birthday, a bonfire party, my plan for a dramatic leap over the flames. I wanted to show him I could do it, and instead I wrecked his birthday, his life. When the branch caught in the wheel of the BMX, I fell down into the fire, and Finn ran into the flames to rescue me, getting burnt himself in the process.

I'll never forgive myself for that.

We stayed together in the hospital for weeks afterward, Finn racing about the corridors in a wheelchair because his feet were burnt and bound up with cling-film stuff to help them heal. My burns took longer to fix. I'd been wearing a T-shirt and my arms, shoulder and neck were burnt, but the worst damage was on the right side of my face, my cheek, my temple, my ear.

Nobody could see the hurt inside, but the scars on my face were clear enough. Luck? That's when I stopped believing in it, end of story.

I looked in the mirror six weeks after the accident and I saw the ridged skin, dark and angry as if it was burning still. When I was eleven they did some skin grafts – Fitz and Chan called me Frankenstein for a while, which was probably designed to toughen me up. It did, a bit.

'There was me thinking you were dead vain because you wouldn't let me mess with your fringe,' Cat says.

'Yeah, right,' I tell her. 'I was probably the first emo kid in London. I've had the fringe since I was eight years old, and I'll still have it when I'm eighty.'

'I like the fringe,' Cat says. 'But you don't have to hide stuff from me.'

I frown, because I'm pretty sure that Cat's hiding something too. Her faraway eyes, the tears that have nothing to do with hay fever or face paint. How much do I really know about her? Not a whole lot.

'I told you my secret,' I say. 'How about yours? You told me everyone has their bad memories, secrets hidden away. So tell me.'

Cat laughs. 'I don't have a secret,' she says.

'No?'

'No. Nothing dark and tragic, anyway. Maybe I said that, but . . .'

'Cat, tell me,' I say. 'It helps to share things, I promise.' This is something I'm only just starting to realize, but all the same, I know it's true. Bringing those bad memories out of the dark takes away their power to hurt you somehow.

Cat sighs and huffs and hugs her knees, silent for a long moment. Then, when I think there's no way she'll ever open up, her sad green eyes lock on to mine.

'I have a brother,' she says at last. 'Josh. He's – ten years old. And he's been ill, very ill, for a long time. But – well, he's better now, and he'll be coming home really, really soon.'

I open my eyes wide. 'Cat,' I say, honestly shocked.

'I didn't even know you had a brother. What's wrong with him? How long has he been ill?'

She just shakes her head, as if she can't trust herself to speak. 'Ages. Years, really. I don't want to talk about it – I just wanted you to know, OK?'

I put an arm round her shoulders, stroke her hair. 'It's not fair, Mouse,' she whispers. 'He's just a little kid. Kids aren't meant to get sick.'

'No, they're not,' I say. 'They're really not.' We sit for a while in silence. It feels like Cat has handed me something special, worth more than stolen chocolates or glow-in-the-dark stars. She's given me a piece of herself. She's not just a beautiful, daring, posh girl any more. She's Cat, acting tough and putting on a brave face when inside she's hurting for her little brother. She snuffles in the dark, wiping a sleeve across her eyes.

'But it's all going to be OK now,' she says brightly. 'Like I said, Josh will be home soon, and we can be a family again. Sorted!'

'I hope so,' I say.

Cat jumps up suddenly, picking up the hot chocolate mugs. 'It's getting late,' she says, suddenly anxious. 'I don't want Mum and Dad to find you here.'

'I'll say I was helping you with your homework,' I grin.

'No, no, you'd best just go. Seriously.' We pad down the stairs together, and suddenly Cat grabs hold of my belt and untucks the forgotten devil's tail, holding it up. 'Sure you're not a bad influence?' she asks.

'Certain,' I tell her. 'That'd be you.'

We hug in the hallway while Lucky sniffs around at our feet.

'Thanks for telling me your secrets,' she whispers. 'And thanks for listening to mine. It helps, y'know?'

'I know,' I say. 'It can't be easy for you, but you know I'll always listen, if you want to talk. Thanks for telling me about the star maps too. You're up there, on my star map. OK?'

Cat laughs. 'What am I, a fleck of light from a faraway galaxy?'

'Something like that.'

I can't tell her the truth, can I? I can't tell her that in my sky, she's the brightest star.

19

Going back to school after an exclusion was never going to be easy, but at least the October break has given people other stuff to think about. Most people, that is.

'You're a hero,' Fitz tells me as we slouch into school. 'A legend. They'll be talking about your graffiti hit for years to come, man.'

'Yeah, right,' Chan says. 'The spelling, the paint on your fingers, the mouse tag in the corner . . . crazy.'

'Thanks, Chan,' I tell him. 'Don't hold back now. Tell it like it is.'

Chan shrugs. 'Just saying.'

The long wall where I painted my graffiti masterpiece has been repainted in flat grey paint, as if it never existed at all, but I had my moment of glory. I saw the kids' faces as they clocked the explosion of colour, the swirls of pattern, the wild, wonderful, glad-to-be-alive graffiti. I smile just thinking about it, my heart singing inside of me.

Mr Brown ambushes me as I slope along the corridor. He hauls me into his office and sits down behind a shiny wooden desk the size of a pool table.

'Those are not school trousers,' he growls, eyeing my skinny black jeans.

'They're *my* school trousers, Sir,' I reply politely.

Mr Brown sighs. 'Kavanagh,' he barks. 'I'd like to believe that you're sorry for the senseless destruction you caused to this school last term. Your letter led me to believe that you were ready to turn over a new leaf. Is that correct?'

Hmmm. I have a feeling it might take more than a new leaf – more like a whole tree. 'Yes, Sir,' I say.

'Good, good,' he says. 'You may not believe this, Kavanagh, but I'm on your side. I want to make Green Vale a better school, a place where teachers and students work together to achieve the very best they can . . . I can't do that without your help.'

I smile and nod and pretend I have a clue what he's talking about.

'I'll be expecting a good report from your teachers on behaviour, attitude and effort,' he goes on. 'You haven't had the best of starts in life, Kavanagh, but don't throw your future away on vandalism and stupidity. Make something of yourself. Show us what you're made of.'

I look at my fingers, spreading them wide. Skin, bone and blood, or stardust?

'You've been given a fresh start – I hope you realize just how lucky you are. Well?' he concludes, narrowing his eyes. 'Is there anything you've been thinking about? Anything you'd like to say to me, in the light of all that's happened?'

I feel like a rabbit caught in the headlights. There are lots of things I'd like to say to Mr Brown – I'm just not sure he's ready to hear them.

'Kavanagh?' he prompts.

'OK,' I say brightly. 'About the wall by the gym . . .'

'Yes, yes?'

'I think you were wrong, that's all. That wall needs some colour. This school needs some colour, and that really shouldn't be a crime. Sir.'

Mr Brown's face turns a startling shade of pink, and his eyes look as though they may pop out of his head. He runs a finger around his collar, as if it's choking him, and his mouth opens and closes, a bit like a goldfish. I can tell he is not impressed by my speech. Slowly, it dawns on me that he wasn't asking for my views and opinions at all. He was waiting for another apology, or for me to thank him for his lenient approach. Oops.

'Well, Sir,' I say, briskly. 'I'd better be going. Don't want to be late for class!'

New leaf? Yeah, right.

Once again, school swallows up my life. It's just the same – sour-faced teachers, grey, crumbling classrooms, stodgy school dinners that lie in your belly like cold gruel.

Then something weird happens. In art, Mr Lewis shows me a vast six foot canvas at the back of the classroom, behind the partition where the art books are. The rest of the class are drawing a still life of dusty wine bottles, in between hurling paper planes about and discussing last night's *Eastenders*.

'It's for you,' Mr Lewis says. 'You like working large, don't you? Let's see what you can do with this.'

I frown. 'Why?' I ask.

'Not my idea,' he grunts. 'Mr Brown thinks you've got something to say, and he wants to see what it is. Brushes and paint, mind, none of that aerosol rubbish.' He stalks away.

I look at the paints and brushes arranged by the sink, then at the big, blank canvas. I don't want to paint on a bright, white background. I am used to peeling bus shelters, pitted brickwork, bleak grey concrete. Mr Brown is wrong. Without those things, I have nothing to say.

There's an old armchair in the book corner, and I sink into it, out of sight behind the shelves. I take a bite of Mars bar and open a book on Van Gogh. I don't read much, but the pictures in this book tell their own story. They're all about colour, about being alive. I read a caption that says Van Gogh sold just one painting during his lifetime. He gave another to a friend, who used it to patch up a hole in his chicken shed.

Maybe it's not so weird for artists to be misunderstood.

Mr Lewis peers round the partition to see what I've done, and looks smugly satisfied that I'm eating chocolate with my feet up on the bookshelf. 'Hmphh,' he says.

Next art lesson, I drag the armchair round so that it sits in front of the big, white canvas. I stare at it all lesson, while the others draw wine bottles, wondering if I have anything to say, and if so, how to say it.

In the third art lesson, I start to draw. I draw a boy, as tall as I am, with a sad face and a Green Vale uniform and a small pirate dog at his heels. Mr Lewis appears and tells me that the legs are too long and the hands are too small. He drags a full-length mirror over from the corner and props it against the bookshelf, and I look and check and fix things up.

Then I start painting, and that takes weeks. I mix black and white acrylic to make a hundred shades of grey, and paint grey skin, grey lips, grey hair, grey clothes with grey folds and creases. Everything is dull and monochrome, like a black-and-white photo in a long-ago album. It takes a whole lesson just to paint one hand, to get the light and shadows just right, to make it look real.

'Interesting,' Mr Lewis says.

When I start on the background, a clashing, crashing explosion of rainbow colour that drips and smudges and splatters over the black-and-white boy, Mr Lewis smiles. I've never seen him do that before. Ever.

Fitz and Chan come up to the art room one lunchtime to check out the painting.

'Spooky,' Fitz says. 'But good, man.'

'You think?'

'You've let all that red drip on to the figure,' Chan points out. 'And what about all those splodges and splatters?'

'It's meant to be like that,' I say. 'Can't you tell?'

Chan pulls a face. 'I'm not really the arty type,' he says.

'I didn't think I was,' I admit. 'Not like this, anyhow. But I want to do another one now – a colour figure with grey all around it, and broken glass and barbed wire and stuff.' As I talk, I wonder if I can actually stick those things on to the painting, like a collage. Maybe graffiti art isn't the only way to say stuff, after all?

'You've gone all highbrow,' Fitz says, thoughtfully. 'It's Cat's influence. Has to be.'

'I don't think so,' I say.

'Still don't know what she sees in you,' Fitz says. 'Pretty, posh girls don't usually go for dates involving chip shops and dog-walking. Posh girls like class. You know – picnics, music, champagne, fireworks. I've seen it on the telly.'

'Yeah?' I grin. 'Last week you were telling me to treat her mean to keep her keen.'

'Well, yeah,' Fitz admits. 'You have to find a balance between the two.'

'Cat's different,' I say. 'She doesn't care about that stuff.'

She's too busy worrying about Josh, for starters. He still isn't home, and every time I ask about him she changes the subject. I have a feeling that maybe things aren't going quite as well as she thinks.

At least things are quiet on the Eden Estate – Scully hasn't reappeared and a trial date has been set for January, which means that maybe he really will go down this time. Lucky isn't missing him, that's for sure – and even Mum has stopped reminding me that Lucky isn't really our dog. It's like he's a part of the family now.

'Romance,' Fitz announces with a flourish, waving a withered old sunflower from the display on the bookshelf in front of my face. 'That's what you need, Mouse, mate. Posh girls like that sort of thing.'

'All girls,' Chan chips in. He has five sisters, so I guess he'd know. 'They like moonlight, and flowers, and surprises.'

Well, Cat likes surprises all right, I know that.

'Where am I going to get picnics, music, champagne, fireworks?' I ask.

'You'll think of something. You gotta make an effort,' Fitz counsels. 'Or . . .'

'Or what?'

'You'll lose her,' he says.

So I plan my surprise, and Fitz and Chan roll their eyes and tell me it's not classy enough, but they agree to help, all the same.

'Wow,' says Cat. 'Wow.'

We are having a picnic on the roof of the only bus shelter on the Eden Estate. A rickety ladder, twined with tinsel, was leaning up against the bus shelter when we arrived, but it's gone now, so we'll have to jump back down. I've spread a couple of old picnic rugs and some pillows across the corrugated steel and set up Fitz's ghetto blaster in the corner. Already, Lucky has snuggled down between us, sighing, as if he lounges about on bus-shelter roofs every day.

'When I was a kid, that summer in the country, there was a tree house,' I tell Cat. 'It was brilliant – you could lie out at night, watching the stars. There are no trees on the Eden Estate, though, so I got a bit of a thing about bus shelters.'

'You're crazy,' Cat laughs.

'You're not?'

I rummage around under the picnic rugs and bring out a bunch of red roses, only slightly wilted. Mr Lewis used them as his still life earlier today – I had to pick chewing gum off one of the roses, and shake pencil sharpenings out of the others.

'Mouse, they're lovely!'

'You like it?' I ask her. 'All this?'

'I love it. We can see everything . . . and nobody even knows we're here!'

She snuggles down against the slanted roof, peeping out over the top. Eden is looking especially gorgeous tonight. Last week someone – not me – painted a vivid sunrise on the long wall opposite, and overnight a scattering of stencilled silver stars sprang up on the cracked concrete around the old playground.

The Phoenix ruins are stuffed with plants, and flowers have started to appear all along the footpath that snakes through the estate. It's almost December, but it's still mild and there've been no frosts. Some of the flowers have been scuffed up, but most are still there. They make old ladies smile and little girls bend down to pick them, and day by day there are more.

'Did your mum do that?' Cat wants to know. 'With the flowers?'

'No. Could be anybody – or lots of people,

maybe. It's like someone looted a garden centre – actually, knowing this place, maybe they did?'

'The copycat graffiti is cool too,' Cat says. 'And the lifts . . .'

Cat and I added metres of silver tinsel to the spray-painted lifts just last week. Eden Estate is changing. It started as a few flowers, a protest about the torching of the Phoenix, but it's turning into more than that. It's about the people turning a sad, grey dump into somewhere less grim, less scary.

A couple of women wander up to the bus stop. We stay quiet, grinning, but although one of them wonders out loud where the music is coming from, they assume it must be from one of the tower block balconies. When the bus comes, a blaze of light sweeping through the estate, they get on without a backward glance. It's only when an old man glances out from a top-deck window that we're spotted. Cat blows him a kiss, and his startled face has us snorting with laughter as the bus swoops off into the night.

A moped putters to a halt below and a carrier bag appears on the edge of the bus shelter roof. Chan's uncle is a pizza delivery man. I ordered cheese and pineapple, with Coke instead of champagne, and Mars bars for afterwards.

'You thought of everything!' Cat laughs. She spots the tail end of my school tie dangling from a pocket where I stuffed it earlier. 'What's this, a tie? If I'd known we were dressing up, I'd have worn my party dress!'

'I like you as you are,' I tell her.

Cat hooks the school tie round my neck and reels me in. 'You too,' she says. 'You're very cute in a tie. Wish I went to your school.'

'You don't, Cat. It's a dump.'

'A cool dump, though,' Cat argues. 'At our school, nothing exciting ever happens. You could die of boredom in assembly one morning and nobody would even notice for hours. It's that exciting.'

'Hmmm,' I say. 'I can see how that might be difficult for you.'

'Maybe I'll ask for a transfer, turn up at your school one of these days . . . that'd be a laugh. Or you could come to mine.'

'Thought you said it was all girls?' I frown.

'It is,' Cat grins. 'Trust me, they'd love you.'

We duck down as a gang of kids swagger past, laughing and clowning around just inches from our heads.

'How's Josh?' I ask, quietly, once the kids have gone. 'Is he any better? I was thinking, if you want, I could come in and meet him. I know how rotten it is to be stuck in hospital –'

'No,' Cat says.

'No?'

'I don't want you to see him like that,' she says softly. 'They're doing more tests before they let him home, but it's just a temporary setback. He'll be home soon – you can meet him then.'

I shrug. 'OK.'

'He'd like you,' Cat says.

'I'd like him, I bet.'

We finish our pizza. In the distance, I can see three shadowy figures moving about in the darkness. One of them gives me a thumbs-up sign – Fitz.

'All that's missing is the stars,' I tell Cat.

'Well, even you can't organize that.'

'You think?'

We look up at the dark, velvet sky, and right on cue, there's a soft, whooshing sound and the darkness explodes into a fountain of tiny white diamonds.

'Oh!' Cat gasps. 'Fireworks! How did you . . .'

I put a finger to her lips as another shower of stars erupts, followed by a couple of rockets, complete with wailing sound effects. Lucky leans against me for reassurance, but he's got used to fireworks – all through November, the kids on the estate have been setting off bangers and rockets every chance they got.

More fountains of light and colour appear, blurring and sinking into the night sky like drops of bright watercolour on wet paper.

In the light from above, I can see Cat's face, tilted up towards the sky, her lips parted, smiling. On the ground, a couple of kids on bikes and a couple walking a dog have stopped to watch the show. On and on the fireworks go, colours drifting, stars fading into nothing, sparks of silver and gold raining down to earth. When it's finally over, there are a few ragged claps, a whistle of approval from the kids on bikes. Cat hugs me.

'Thanks,' she whispers. 'That was the coolest thing, Mouse. The best night ever.'

Lucky and I walk Cat home, then slouch back across the estate just after eleven. It's quiet now, with a soft drizzle starting to fall, and we're mooching past Eagle Heights when suddenly, Lucky sits down in the middle of the footpath and refuses to move. I tug his washing-line lead, try to reason with him.

'C'mon. What's the problem? You can't just stop!'

I tug on the lead again, but Lucky digs his heels in, leaning back stubbornly. He has never been disobedient or awkward before. His eyes look wild and anxious, and his grin has slipped into a lopsided grimace.

'We're nearly home,' I tell him. 'Come on!' The air smells of fireworks, but I can't see anything that would spook Lucky. The estate is quiet – unusually quiet. 'Lucky, come on!'

Still he won't move. I bend down and pick him up, but he struggles, his little legs scrabbling against me as if trying to escape from an unseen enemy.

'Shh,' I tell him, holding him tight as I walk on.

Suddenly there's a movement just ahead of me, and a rough voice calls out, 'Hey, stupid!'

I keep walking, head down, a little bit faster, but a stooped, scrawny figure steps out from the shadows, a can of beer in his tattooed hand. 'Hello, Mouse,' says Scully. 'Long time no see.'

'I thought . . .'

'That I was still in the nick?' he sneers. 'Well, I was, of course, thanks to your mum. But I'm out now – I got bail. And I'm not happy, Mouse. I'm not happy at all.'

I take a step back, but Scully grabs on to my sleeve. He's right up in my face, his eyes bloodshot, his chin dark with stubble, snarling. He's stronger than he looks. I can feel his breath, sour and stale against my skin, and I remember that this guy carries a knife. Lucky is crying now, a high-pitched whimper, his whole body wriggling and writhing to get free.

'Thief!' Scully hisses, and a fleck of spit lands on my cheek. A couple of kids walking past keep their eyes firmly on the gutter, keen to stay out of trouble. I don't blame them. I'm keen to stay out of trouble too, yet here it is, staring me in the face.

'D'you hear me?' Scully yells. 'D'you freakin' hear me? You nicked my dog!'

'I didn't,' I argue. 'I found him, on Clapham High Street. He was in an accident. I knew he wasn't mine, but I thought I'd hold on to him for you, while you were away . . .'

Lucky stops struggling and lies still in my arms, like he knows I just betrayed him. Scully grabs on to his neckerchief, and the little pirate dog bares his teeth, shuddering so hard his whole body shakes. Whatever I told Mum, whatever I said to Scully, there's no way I can give Lucky up. I just can't.

'I can keep hold of him, if you like,' I say, my voice calm and low. 'Till everything's sorted out. You don't need the hassle of looking after a dog, not at a time like this.'

Scully leans into my face. 'You're right, kid,' he snarls. 'Times are bad. Still, my mates have had a gentle word with a couple of the witnesses – Mark and JJ – and it turns out they don't remember much at all about what happened at the Phoenix. They've withdrawn their statements. That's good news, yeah?'

'Yeah,' I echo, dully. 'Good news for you.'

'I reckon your mum might be better off keeping her mouth shut too. She really doesn't want to get mixed up in a court case. Messy business. You can tell your mum that, from me.'

I swallow, nodding. 'I'll tell her.'

'I bet you've got to like my dog,' Scully says. 'While I've been away. Maybe you'd like to keep him?'

'Yes. I'd like that.'

'I wouldn't miss him,' he says. 'Lousy little mongrel, always whining and moaning. Nothin' but trouble. But he's my dog, see. I have a responsibility.'

Scully laughs. He wrenches Lucky from me and drops him on to the pavement, where he darts behind my legs, whimpering. 'Let's see, shall we? Let's see where the little rat really wants to be? We'll let him choose.'

I stare down at Lucky, and he gazes back at me, terrified.

Scully takes a step back, into the shadows. 'C'mon, stupid,' he says, his voice cold and hard. 'C'mon, boy.'

Lucky steps out from behind my legs, takes a step towards Scully. 'Lucky, here,' I say, but he doesn't seem to hear me. He slinks forward, his body hunched, shivering, like he's walking to the gallows.

'OK, stupid,' Scully says. 'OK.'

And finally I get it; Stupid is Lucky's real name.

'Lucky!' I plead, but the little pirate dog doesn't

look round. He walks right up to Scully, who jabs him with the toe of his trainer and makes him yelp. Lucky runs behind him, cowering.

I don't get it. I don't understand why any dog would go back to someone who treats him like dirt. 'Push off then, kid!' Scully yells. 'Your little mutt don't want you any more, OK? He knows where he belongs. And don't forget to tell your mum I'm out – and I'm watching her!'

He chucks his empty can at me. It hits my leg, spilling dregs of stale beer down my jeans. I stand still on the pavement, staring at Lucky. He stares back, lost, shivering, his eyes huge. He's not grinning. He may never grin again. Then he turns after Scully and disappears into the night.

There's a light on in Jake's workshop and I hammer on the door until he unlocks it, opening it a crack. 'Mouse?' he says, frowning. 'What's up, kid?'

'Can I come in?'

Jake holds the door wide and I slip inside. 'So. Girlfriend like the fireworks?'

I nod woodenly, but the rooftop picnic seems about a million years ago. All I can think about is Lucky – how he abandoned me to be with some thug who calls him Stupid. How I abandoned him.

'I've got a problem,' I blurt out. 'A big problem, Jake.'

'Yeah?'

'Scully,' I say.

'Ah.' Jake puts the kettle on, spoons out dried milk and coffee. 'I heard he was back.'

It all pours out then, about the threats to Mum, about Lucky choosing Scully over me. 'Why did he do that?' I demand. 'Why would he leave me for that jerk? I've never been mean to him. I've made sure he was fed, walked him twice a day, let him sleep on the end of my bed. So why?'

Jake shrugs. 'Dogs are loyal,' he tells me. 'Scully had Stupid – sorry, Lucky – from a pup. Dog probably felt like he didn't have a choice.'

'Scully doesn't even care about Lucky,' I say.

'Maybe not,' Jake agrees. 'But he's Scully's dog – you knew that right from the start. I'm not saying it's fair, Mouse, but there's not a whole lot you can do.'

I blow on my coffee, drinking it slowly. I think about Lucky and Scully and I think about me and my dad, and I wonder how come the people who are supposed to love and look after us can sometimes let us down so badly. Like Lucky, I know I'd go to Dad in a minute if he picked up the phone and asked me to, or wrote, or turned up out of the blue. He won't, though. He doesn't love me enough, and there's nothing I can do about that.

Maybe it's better that way.

'Scully's going to get away with it, isn't he?' I ask. 'The drug-pushing, the knife threat, all of it.'

Jake sighs.

'I don't know, Mouse,' he says.

In the lobby of Nightingale House, a couple of strings of icicle lights have appeared, draped across the ceiling. It looks cool, and it's dimmer than the strip light, so you can't see the peeling paint or the empty fag packets in the corner. An hour ago, they'd have made me smile, made me think that things were changing for the better. Now, I know that things will never change.

Up on the ninth floor, I turn the key in the lock at number 114. It's a moment before I realize that Mum is sitting in the living room in the dark, under the leafy plants. I switch the light on.

'Mum?' I say. 'Are you OK?'

She looks up, arranging her face into a smile that doesn't fool anyone.

'Jake just rang,' she says, her voice sad and heavy. 'He told me about Scully – and about Lucky. I'm sorry, Mouse.'

I sink down beside her. 'I'll get Lucky back,' I say. 'I have to.'

Mum bites her lip. 'I think maybe you should leave it. We've known all along that Lucky was Scully's dog. Try taking him back and you'll make even more of an enemy of Scully – and Mouse, we really don't need that.'

I have a feeling it's kind of too late for that. 'He told me to say he'd be watching you,' I say. 'Already his mates have got Mark and JJ to take back their police statements – that means you're the only witness, Mum. People would understand if you chose not to go to court. Nobody'd blame you . . .'

'I'm going to testify,' Mum says calmly. 'It's the right thing to do.'

I feel cold all over. If Scully's mates decide to have a 'talk' with Mum – well, she's not the kind to back down easily. And that spells trouble.

A handpainted paper banner emblazoned with the words *reach for the stars* has been draped across the school corridor, just along from Mr Brown's office. Wonky stars snipped from gold foil paper are collaged across it, plus a sprinkling of silver glitter. This is odd. We are not usually asked to reach for anything at Green Vale Comp, unless it's a plate of chips in the school canteen or a rope swing in the gym. Stars? Yeah, right. Looks like Mr Brown has finally lost it.

'Kavanagh!' yells the man himself, through the

scrum of early morning pupils. He is waving his arms around like a drowning man, and his face has that desperate, manic glare that all teachers at Green Vale develop after a while.

'What've you done now?' Fitz asks, impressed. 'Sounds like trouble!'

'Where's your tie?' Chan asks.

'Dangling from a bus shelter roof on the Eden Estate,' I snap. 'OK?'

I couldn't find my tie this morning, but that's the least of my troubles. I'm trying so hard to hold it all together today that I really don't think I can face a telling off from Mr Brown. I keep on walking.

'MARTIN KAVANAGH!' he roars again. 'I want to see you! My office, breaktime!'

'Everything OK?' Fitz asks, as we file into class. 'You seem kind of touchy.'

'I'm fine,' I snarl. 'Just leave it.' I can't even get my head round what happened last night, let alone explain it to Fitz and Chan. Not yet, anyway.

'Girl trouble,' I hear them mutter. 'Miaow!'

At breaktime, I hide out in the art room to avoid Mr Brown, then slouch over to the Learning Support Unit. This is the low point of my week. It's where they put the kids who don't speak English too well yet, or the ones like me who have dyslexia and problems with reading, writing and spelling.

Our regular teacher has been off work for months with stress-related depression, so we have an endless stream of supply teachers instead. Sometimes they are keen and well-meaning. Mostly they couldn't care less.

Three Polish girls in the corner are playing Junior Scrabble, which is kind of educational, only I think they're playing it in Polish. Kiran Jamal is drawing rude pictures on the desk, and Ceri Lloyd is touching up her peach-coloured lipstick. The supply teacher pretends not to notice, even when paper planes and chewing-gum wrappers sail above his head.

I slump across the table, doodling stars and spirals across a worksheet illustrated with cartoons. It looks like it was designed for a six-year-old, and I bet most six-year-olds would have it finished by now too. I've barely started. So what? My life's a mess, and one unfinished worksheet won't make a bit of difference.

There's a loud knock on the door, and everyone turns to look as a girl walks in, a pretty, mixed-race girl with ringlet curls and slanting eyes. She's wearing a short black skirt, a little white shirt and a Green Vale Comp tie with the end all frayed and worn, exactly like the one I lost last night. My jaw drops so far it just about hits the tabletop.

It's Cat.

She gives me a little wave and winks and grins, and the boys at the back gawp and make wolf-whistle noises under their breath.

'Can I help you?' the supply teacher asks.

'My name is Catrin Thomas and I just started at Green Vale today. I'm supposed to be working here?'

'Oh? I'm afraid I don't know anything about that. I don't know –'

'I'll just sit here, shall I?' Cat says, nodding towards my desk. 'Do one of these worksheets, see how I get on. Yeah?'

'Sit with us,' the boys at the back leer. 'We can show you everything you need to know! Stay away from Kavanagh, he's weird.'

'Just my type.' She smiles sweetly and slides into the seat beside me. 'Surprise!' she says.

Surprise? It's that, all right. I try to dredge up a smile, but fail. My chest feels tight, and my hands have clenched into fists. It's not a good surprise, that's for sure. 'What are you playing at?' I hiss.

'Schools,' Cat says. 'Isn't it obvious?'

'You're wearing my tie,' I accuse.

'Well, they weren't going to let just anyone in, were they? I had to look the part. You wouldn't believe the trouble I went to pull this off. I had to fake phone calls from my mum, and from the education authority in Cardiff –'

'Cardiff?'

'We just moved here from Cardiff,' she says sweetly. 'At the weekend. All my files got lost in the post.'

'Do you go to drama club, or a support group for compulsive liars?'

'Acting, lying, it's all the same thing,' Cat says. 'Anyway, I'm here. Cool, huh?'

'No,' I say through gritted teeth. 'Not cool. I told you, Cat, I'm trying to stay out of trouble – I don't need this.'

'I'm not causing trouble,' she says airily. 'Just having a laugh. What're you doing in this class, anyhow?' She lowers her voice. 'I mean, it's not like you're thick, is it?'

That hurts. 'Thanks a bunch,' I say. 'But apparently I am. My spelling's bad, my reading's worse, and writing gives me a headache.'

'This'd give anyone a headache,' Cat replies. 'They'll be dancing on the tables, next.'

'You wanted to see what it was like.'

'I know.' She grins. 'It's even better than I imagined. Our place is the opposite – super-strict. Sneeze in class and you get detention for a week.'

'Funny how well you're adapting.'

'Isn't it? Maybe I'm just born to be bad. So. What're you doing?'

She picks up the cartoony worksheet. Her eyes widen a little when she sees the questions, but she doesn't say anything, and I can feel my skin flush crimson. Is she laughing at me, or pitying me? I don't know which would feel worse.

'You're dyslexic, aren't you?' she says to me. 'Lots of people are. My friend Naomi . . .'

I don't want to hear about Cat's friend Naomi. I pick up the worksheet, scrunch it up into a ball and skim it across the classroom. The supply teacher looks nervous, but doesn't say anything. I look at the clock. Five minutes till lunchtime. I don't know if I can survive it.

'It took me forever to track you down,' Cat is saying, brightly. 'I went to maths, French, history, chemistry . . .'

I hide behind my fringe, scowling.

She frowns. 'Aren't you even a little bit glad to see me, Mouse? I thought you'd be pleased. I thought this would make you laugh!'

'Did you?'

'Don't be mad at me, Mouse,' she says.

The bell goes, and kids stampede for the door. I grab my bag and try to lose myself in the crowd, but Cat is running along behind me. 'So,' she asks me. 'What happens at lunch?'

I don't even want to think about that. Fitz, Chan, Neela Rehman, the rest of the kids in my class – and

Cat, eating turkey twizzlers and pretending it's cool. It doesn't bear thinking about. Help me, I think. Please.

A firm hand grasps the back of my jacket and pulls me up short.

'Kavanagh,' Mr Brown says. 'Finally. My office now.'

Sometimes, help comes from the most unexpected places.

I sit across the desk from Mr Brown. 'No tie today, Kavanagh?' he asks.

I could tell him it was stolen by a psycho posh girl who is in the school canteen right now, impersonating a Green Vale pupil and asking the dinner ladies if they have Camembert cheese and fairly traded chocolate pudding, but a few dregs of loyalty linger on.

'Lost it,' I say.

'I'm impressed,' Mr Brown says.

'Uh?'

'Not about the tie,' he says, hastily. 'No. It's the effort you've been making to stay out of trouble, and the wonderful things you've been doing in art. Mr Lewis has nothing but praise for you.'

'He does?'

'He does. And I have to say I agree. You have an unusual talent.'

'Who, me?' I can feel myself sitting up straighter, taller.

'Yes, you,' Mr Brown says. 'What's more, I feel I may have underestimated the depth of your feelings with that whole graffiti incident. I've reread your letter and I can see that you raised some very real criticisms. What seemed like an act of vandalism at the time may have been, in fact, a cry from the heart.'

He's crazy. Teachers get this way, sometimes, especially at this time of year. Stress, school dinners and endless school reports have scrambled his brains.

'You made a valid point with your graffiti protest. I don't approve of the way you made it, but you were right. This school needs more colour. That wall needs more colour! A mural, perhaps? Something tasteful – perhaps a countryside scene? You're the expert, of course. I thought you might find time to draw up some designs over the Christmas break?'

I blink.

'Green Vale has always been a school where pupils are encouraged to reach for the stars,' he says. 'This is your chance to do just that!'

I really scare Mr Brown then. I jump up and give him a high five, tell him he's not the stuffy old loser everyone says he is. Then I'm out of there, sprinting off along the corridor, jumping up to drag down the paper banner as I go. It falls to the ground behind me, curling itself around Mr Brown's feet. Amazingly, he doesn't seem to mind.

At least one thing is going right today.

My fingers are gritty with silver glitter from the banner, like they are made of stars. I might even put Mr Brown up on my star map – a distant star, obviously, in a far-off galaxy. But still.

The minute I get to the school canteen, though, my mood crashes. Cat is at a table with Fitz, Chan and a whole bunch of Year Nine lads. She's laughing, flicking her hair, flirting shamelessly with Lee Costa who is perched on the table beside her, eating her chips.

She sees me and waves, winking cheekily. Suddenly, I'm not hungry any more. I turn round and walk away, but Cat is right behind me. 'Wait up,' she says. 'What did he want with you, the Head? Are you in trouble?'

'No,' I say shortly. 'You are.'

'What?'

'You don't belong here,' I snap, though it's clear from what I've just seen that she's settled in pretty well.

She slips a hand into mine, but I shake her off. 'Mouse, what's wrong?' she asks, genuinely baffled.

I stop walking and turn to face her. Last night, holed up on the bus-shelter roof watching fireworks explode above the Eden Estate, I felt closer to Cat than I've ever felt to anyone. Today, it's like I never knew her at all.

'Why did you come here, Cat?' I ask. 'To laugh at me? To see what school is like if you don't have rich parents and endless cash? To land me in trouble again? To flirt with my friends, sneer at the scabby desks and scruffy classrooms?'

'It's not like that,' Cat says in a small voice.

'So what is it like?' I demand. 'Oh, what's the point? I'm sick of your stupid games. Go away and leave me alone.'

I think she might cry, but instead her eyes flash with anger and she pushes past me, shoving her way through the double doors and marching out across the playground.

'I want my tie back,' I yell after her. She just drags it off and drops it on to the concrete playground without a backward glance.

'Sheesh,' says Fitz from behind me. 'Great move, Mouse. You've really blown it now.'

I never used to have a girlfriend and I never used to have a dog, but now, without them, I am lost.

I feel bad about Cat. She wasn't trying to wind me up, but the sight of her flirting with Lee Costa was just about the last straw. I got mad, and I said stuff I shouldn't have said, and she walked out of my life. It's probably a good thing. She doesn't need a boyfriend from the Eden Estate, especially one who is sad and scared and has enemies like Frank Scully.

All the same, I miss her.

I walk up and down her street about a dozen times that night, and again the night after. She doesn't come out, but on the third night, her mum pulls back the curtain and gives me a long, hard stare.

I give up then, pretty much. Looks like I'm destined to be a no-dog, no-girl boy. I try to walk away, but walking away from Cat is not easy. I get about halfway down the street, come to a halt at a bus stop and look back at her house. If she'd just come out, then maybe I could explain, tell her why I acted so mean. Maybe.

I have a quick look around, then haul myself up on to the bus-stop roof. The view is better from up here, but it's dark and cold and there's a soft drizzle starting to fall. I've just about given up hope when I spot a bicycle whirling along towards me, ridden by a sad-faced girl with coffee-coloured skin and ringlet curls.

I jump down off the bus shelter roof. 'Cat!'

She skids her bike to a halt and the dynamo lights fizzle and fade. 'You,' she says, coldly.

'Nice to see you too. Look, Cat, about the other day . . .'

She shrugs. 'I'll get over it. You're not so special.'

That hurts.

'You walked past my house about a million times last night,' she comments. 'Why didn't you call in?'

'Didn't think you'd want to see me. Why didn't you come down?'

'Same reason.' Her mouth twitches into a smile. 'You look terrible.'

'Of course I do! I've lost you, I've lost Lucky and there's a knife-wielding maniac on the loose out there with a grudge against my mum . . . I've had better weeks.'

Cat's eyes widen. 'What?' she says. 'What are you talking about? What maniac? Where's Lucky?'

We lean against the bus stop and I tell her the whole sorry story. 'Scully doesn't want Lucky,' I explain. 'He just wants to hurt me – and Mum. What if he does something bad to Lucky, just to spite us?'

Cat bites her lip. 'Look, Mouse, this isn't right. We have to get Lucky back!'

My heart leaps, but I know it's not that simple. 'That'll just make Scully madder than ever,' I say sadly. 'Lucky is his dog . . . well, he thinks so, anyway. No. It's awful, but we have to let Lucky go.' Even as I say it, I feel a stab of pain inside. Letting Lucky go is against every instinct I know.

'We can't!' Cat protests.

'If we take Lucky back, Scully's going to go crazy,' I say. 'He's already had a go at the other witnesses, scared them into withdrawing their statements. I don't want him to start on Mum.'

Cat looks let down, as if I just sold my best friend into slavery. Well, maybe I did. I don't know what to do with the mess of anger and frustration and hurt that's bubbling away inside me. I want to kick through plate-glass windows until the pavement glitters with splintered glass, punch a wall until the skin on my fist is mashed and bleeding. I want to yell and swear and curl up and cry.

I don't do any of that, of course. Cat slips her hand into mine.

'What a mess,' she says.

I'd feel better if I could at least see Lucky out and about around the estate, but it's like he has vanished off the face of the earth. Fitz and Chan ask around a bit for me, but nobody's seen Lucky – or Scully – for days.

'Word is that Scully's gone away for a while,' I tell Mum. 'He must be lying low.'

'That's good, isn't it?' Mum asks.

'I suppose.'

I can't stop worrying, though. I just need to know that Lucky is safe. On Friday, after school, I see old Mrs S. carrying her shopping towards the lift, beneath the twinkling icicle lights, and I run up to help.

'Oh, Mouse, thank you,' she says. 'Those bags were heavy! I've been getting a bit of shopping in for my Frank.'

'Right,' I say carefully. 'I heard he was back.'

'Yes,' she says, beaming. 'It was all a mix-up, Mouse. He's not really a bad boy.'

I bite my tongue. Scully has been trouble since the day he was born, I reckon. He may wriggle out of the drug-pushing charge now that he's 'persuaded' the witnesses to back off, but everyone in the Phoenix saw him threaten Mum with a knife. He won't get away with that, surely?

'I've already made some cakes,' Mrs S. is telling me. 'My Frankie has always had a sweet tooth. He's bound to be round to see his old gran.'

We step out of the tinselled lift. 'You haven't seen him yet then?' I press.

'No,' Mrs S. admits. 'He's been over in Luton, the last few days, seeing his mum. He'll be back soon, though – today, perhaps. I want to be ready.'

She turns the key and steps back to let me into the flat. In the lounge, the table is spread as if for a child's party, with plates of iced cakes wrapped in cling film, wilted sandwiches cut into neat triangles and a bottle of lemonade. It looks like Mrs S. has been ready for Frankie's visit for a while.

'I can make some fresh sandwiches now,' she says, taking the shopping bags from me. 'Thank you, Mouse. Would you like some cake? There's plenty!'

'No, no, it's OK,' I tell her. 'Mrs S. . . . well, I hope you don't mind me asking, but did Scully – I mean, Frank – take Lucky to Luton, d'you know? My dog? It turns out he belonged to Frank after all. He – um – took Lucky back, and I miss him, and I just want to know that he's OK.'

'Your dog?' she echoes. 'Oh dear. My Josie didn't say anything about a dog.'

I frown. 'Right. OK,' I say. 'I expect someone around here is looking after Lucky then.'

Mrs S. looks doubtful. 'Maybe,' she says. 'I hope so. I'll have a word with Frank for you, when I do see him. He's just not cut out to look after a dog – his temper gets the better of him.'

My heart sinks to the soles of my converse trainers. Where the heck is Lucky, if he's not with Scully? And what does she mean, about Scully's temper getting the better of him?

'When will Scully – I mean Frank – be back?' I ask.

Mrs S. looks vague. 'Oh, sometime soon, I expect,' she says. 'Today or tomorrow, or maybe the day after. He's bound to come and see me, the minute he can. I'll ask about the dog, I promise.'

'Well, great,' I tell her. 'Thank you.'

Back at the flat, Mum is draping fairy lights round the Swiss cheese plant, singing to herself. 'Bit early, aren't you?' I ask. 'It's not even December till next week.'

'I know, I know, but I thought it might look nice . . . I've had a bit of good news, Mouse.'

I don't want good news when all I can think about is Lucky, alone maybe, hungry, unwanted, unloved. 'Yeah?' I ask.

'Yeah!' Mum grins. 'Julie's been in talks with the council all week, and it looks like they're going to fund some improvements on the Eden Estate . . .'

'Improvements?'

'General repairs, for starters,' Mum explains. 'Which has to be good, because let's face it, most of the flats around here are in a pretty dismal state. It's not just that, though. They're going to build a children's nursery, a youth club and a day centre for senior citizens, down where the Phoenix used to be. And they're going to lease one of the new buildings to us, so that the Phoenix can carry on helping to fight back against the drug problems here on the estate. We'll be back in business, Mouse! Isn't that fantastic?'

'Great,' I say. 'Really, Mum, it's brilliant!'

'We won't just be a small-time charity, working alone,' she tells me. 'We'll be working alongside the council, with proper support from the social services and the health authority. The Phoenix is going be bigger and better than ever!'

I force a smile. 'I'm really glad,' I tell her. 'You've worked so hard on this project, you and Luke and Julie. It's great the council can see that – that they're prepared to help.'

'There's a scheme like this in Liverpool, apparently, where the council are working alongside an anti-drugs charity to clean up a troubled estate,' Mum says. 'So far, the results have been really positive. Julie thinks we should go up north, take a look at how that project is going – get an idea of how we can make it work here.'

'Great,' I echo. Mum turns back to the fairy lights, singing under her breath. For the first time in weeks she looks really happy, her face alive with plans for the future.

'We'll still have a garden,' she tells me. 'The council loved that idea – they want to make it a big community garden, a focal point, with the buildings clustered around it. It's all about creating a sense of identity and belonging for the people here on Eden – helping them to feel part of a community. I've got so many plans!'

I smile, and Mum doesn't notice that it's a thin, sad kind of a smile. Now isn't the time to tell her what Mrs S. said about Scully's temper, or ask about where Lucky can be. She's had enough doom and gloom, lately. I don't want to spoil her optimism.

'Got homework,' I say, dragging my rucksack through to my room. Mum doesn't even raise an eyebrow, although it must be the first time in living memory I've admitted to having homework, let alone threatened to actually do it. I shut the door and flop down on the bed, looking at the ceiling of stars. I think of Mr Brown's mural idea, of the banner with its gold-foil constellations. I think of the council's plans to drag the Eden Estate out of trouble with a coat of paint, a new youth centre and a community garden, to turn it into a place where people can hope.

Then I think of Lucky, whimpering, lost, forgotten already by the bloke who thinks he owns him. If he's not in Luton with Scully, where is he? Curled up in the corner of some lowlife's flat, cringing, scared? He's not OK, I know he's not. I can feel it inside, a sad, sick feeling in the pit of my belly.

Mum's dreaming of a brand-new Phoenix, a brand-new Eden. Me, I'm still stuck in the real world.

Next morning, Saturday, I'm washing cars for Jake to help pay him back for the firework display. I have a date with Cat for later, but even the thought of that can't cheer me up. I barely slept last night, thinking about Lucky. I know – I just know – that he's in trouble.

Fitz and Chan arrive. They know about Lucky and Scully now, so I fill them in on what Mrs S. said yesterday. I explain that Lucky is not with Scully, and how Mrs S. thinks Scully isn't suited to keeping a dog. 'That's his own gran talking,' I remind them. 'If she thinks that, it must be bad.'

'Creep's not fit to look after a stick insect, let alone a dog,' Fitz says.

'You don't think he'd have left Lucky alone?' I wonder out loud. 'Forgotten about him, maybe?'

Jake looks across from the car he's working on, frowning. Fitz lowers his voice. 'Nah' he says. 'He'll have left him with a mate, most likely. We could take a look around, try and find out.'

'Yeah?'

Chan narrows his eyes. 'We can say we've started a dog-walking business,' he says. 'We can pretend we're making lists and rotas for the business, find out about every dog on the estate.'

'Nice one,' Fitz grins.

Jake straightens up, wiping his hands on an oily rag. 'It's not a game,' he says to us. 'Don't go stirring up trouble, OK? I mean it.'

Fitz shrugs. 'We're not doing nothin' wrong,' he says. 'Just getting some facts together. Wassup with that?'

'Don't mess with Frank Scully,' Jake insists.

'We won't,' Fitz says. 'Scully's not here anyway. We'll stay out of trouble, OK, man?'

Fitz and Chan head off, and Jake rolls his eyes. 'Like kids playing at spies,' he huffs. 'Seriously, Mouse, you have to forget about this dog.'

'I can't!' I burst out. 'Not until I know if he's OK or not. Why would Scully nick his dog back and then disappear and leave him behind? It doesn't make sense. I'm worried.'

Jake pushes a hand through his hair, leaving a couple of streaks of grime on his forehead.

'Lucky was mine,' I explain. 'It's not my fault that he was Scully's first. I care about him, OK?'

Jake sighs. 'The dog's all right,' he says.

'You don't know that!'

'I do,' Jake says. 'All right? Scully's got some business deal, down Luton way. He couldn't take the dog, but Lucky's safe, take my word for it. You can relax.'

I open my eyes wide, but Jake can't quite meet my gaze.

'You knew?' I ask. 'You knew he was safe, all this time?'

'I can't get involved in this, Mouse, mate,' Jake says. 'Forget I said anything, yeah?'

I can't believe what I'm hearing. 'Forget?' I echo. 'Jake, you know how worried I've been about Lucky. Now you're saying you knew all along where he was?'

'I'm not saying that,' Jake snaps.

'But you knew he was safe. You knew he was being looked after, fed, cared for. You could have told me!'

'Mouse, mate,' he says through gritted teeth. 'I've said way more than I should have already. Just drop it. You've got cars to wash.'

He walks away, holes up in the little office and slams the door behind him. I can see him through the glass, hunched over the desk, working through a mound of paperwork. His jaw is set, his face angry, but I can't tell whether he's angry with Scully or with me, or maybe even himself.

I head for the sink, fill a fresh bucket with warm

water and add a capful of carwash, grab a sponge and a squeegee and a chamois leather. I wash four cars, one after the other, but it doesn't quite kill the anger, the sense of betrayal. How come Jake knows so much, anyway? I dig out the chrome cleaner and start scrubbing at the chrome trim, polishing so hard I can see my reflection in the silvery surface. Jake comes up behind me, quietly. 'OK,' he says. 'OK, Mouse. I'm sorry.'

'You should have told me, Jake.'

'I know, Mouse, mate,' he says. 'It's complicated, but yeah, I should have told you. Scully's out of order on this.'

'Is he your friend?' I ask, my mouth curled into a sneer. 'Or just a business associate?'

'Don't matter,' Jake tells me. 'Do you want this blasted dog back, or not?'

My heart leaps. 'Yes,' I say. 'You know I do!'

Jake chews his lip. 'Mouse, you have to keep quiet about this,' he says. 'If Scully ever finds out I helped you . . .'

'He won't,' I promise. 'I won't tell anyone, not ever!'

Jake sighs. 'He'll know anyhow,' he says heavily. 'It ain't rocket science. We're gonna have to lie low for a bit, the pair of us.'

'Whatever,' I say.

He walks back to the office, opens a locked

drawer and pulls out a small silver key on a knotted loop of string. 'Come on then.'

We head out across the courtyard, walking down towards the lock-up garages. 'Scully wanted a guard dog, not a pet,' Jake tells me. 'Something fierce, something tough. Then he won Stupid in a card game. It seemed perfect, only the pup grew up small and skinny and about as fierce and tough as ice cream and jelly. Scully wasn't pleased. He didn't treat the dog well – said he was trying to toughen it up.'

Not treating a dog well . . . I try not to think about what that might mean.

'Then Stupid – Lucky, I mean – ran away. Everyone knew it was because he'd treated the dog so badly, but Scully tried to make out the dog had been stolen. Maybe he even believed it himself.'

We're in the lane of lock-up garages now, walking over broken glass, between rows of ancient, ramshackle garages.

'I'm only doing this because I think it's wrong, OK, to leave him alone like this,' Jake is telling me. 'Scully was only meant to be gone overnight, but the deal's taking a while to sort out –'

'Where is he?' I ask, my heart thumping. 'Where's Lucky?'

'I went in and fed him, yesterday, OK?' Jake tells me. 'I've got a spare key, y'see. I swear I wouldn't have let him stay there another night, Mouse. It's wrong. It's cruel.'

Jake stops beside one of the lock-ups, fits the little silver key into the lock. I think I hear a faint whimpering sound, and then Jake is pulling the metal door up and over our heads.

It's dark inside the garage, and it takes me a moment to focus. Down at the back, behind a posh blue car and a tower of piled-up boxes half-hidden in canvas tarpaulin, Lucky is tied to the wall by his washing-line lead. He has pulled so hard to free himself that the neckerchief has turned into a noose round his neck, almost choking him. He has no food, an empty water bowl, nothing but an oily rag to lie on. There is a yellow puddle at his feet, dog dirt in the corner, the stink of ammonia and fear.

I hate Scully so much right then, I could kill him.

'I had to leave him tied up,' Jake says. 'If Scully had come back and found him untied . . . well, don't matter now, I guess.'

'Did you give him the rag to lie on?' I ask. 'The water bowl?'

'Yeah, but it wasn't enough,' Jake says, sadly. 'I should have done more. I'm sorry, Mouse.'

I'm sorry too. I always thought Jake was someone strong, someone I could trust, but I can see now he's just as scared as the rest of us. At least, in the end, he did what was right. Another day like this and Lucky could have died, maybe, sad and starving and shivering in the long, cold nights.

Jake bends down, slicing through the neckerchief with a penknife. Lucky springs forward, into my arms, and I hide my face against his shivering body. Boys don't cry.

Back at the flat, I make a nest for Lucky beneath the Swiss cheese plant with the twinkling fairy lights. I cover him with my old hoodie, let him lap water from a bowl lifted up to him, take slices of ham from my fingers. He drinks and eats and sleeps a lot, then wakes and gazes at me with sad brown eyes. His lips twitch into a grin.

'He'll be OK,' Mum tells me. 'Thank goodness you found him in time.'

'I couldn't leave him there,' I tell her. 'I just couldn't, Mum.'

'I know, Mouse,' she says. 'I know.'

I told her that I was walking past the lock-ups and heard a whining, scrabbling noise. I pretended I'd been able to force the lock, because I didn't want to dump Jake in trouble. He'll have enough of that on his plate when Scully gets back and finds Lucky gone.

Me too.

'What are we going to do?' I ask Mum.

'Lie low,' she says. 'Stick together. Hope for the best.'

I meet Cat beneath a street light at the corner of her street. 'So, Lucky's back,' she says, her eyes dancing. 'Mouse, I'm so, so glad!'

'Me too,' I tell her. 'But Scully'll go crazy when he finds out. He's still away, so we're OK for now, but things could get very nasty . . .'

'He's on bail,' Cat scoffs. 'What can he do? Besides, you could get the RSPCA on to him. Sick loser. It'll be OK, Mouse, trust me.'

Somehow, I don't think either bail or the threat of the RSPCA would worry Scully much, but I keep my mouth shut.

'Can't wait to see Lucky,' Cat is saying. 'Poor little thing . . .'

'He's much better,' I tell her. 'He was pretty rough at first, but he slept for hours and he's eaten his body weight in ham and sausages and digestive biscuits.'

'I've bought him some Camembert,' Cat says. 'He likes that.'

As we turn in to the estate, we meet Fitz and Chan being towed along by two huge Rottweilers. 'Mouse, man,' Fitz accuses. 'This is all your fault! The dog-walking business was just meant to be a scam, but you try saying no to a nutter like Psycho

Sam. He's signed us up to walk his dogs twice a day from now until Christmas!'

I laugh. 'Think of the money you'll earn.'

'What money?' Fitz wails. 'He reckons it's compensation for the time we broke his window playing footy. Man, we were eight years old! That's harsh!'

'I found Lucky,' I tell them, launching into the edited version of the story I've already told Mum and Cat, the version that doesn't include Jake.

Fitz and Chan high five us, then get dragged off by the lumbering Rottweilers. Cat and I walk between the tower blocks, past the beaten-up kids' playground towards the Phoenix wreckage. I tell her Mum's news about the council's promise to help them rebuild.

'Things are really changing around here,' Cat says. 'It starts with a few graffiti hits and a couple of flowers planted in the ashes, and now look at what's happening!'

'Yeah . . .' I'm looking at something else, though, something just beyond the wrecked Phoenix, a shiny, dark blue VW camper van painted with millions of tiny silver stars.

It reminds me of another van, a clapped-out patchwork-painted VW, a van from the past, from the summer I spent with my dad. It makes me think of Finn, Dizzy and Leggit, of festival nights curled up on a thin bunk, of hot apple squash made from the ancient whistling kettle and drunk scalding hot from spotty tin mugs.

'See that old van?' I start saying to Cat, and then everything goes crazy because a big, scruffy black-and-white wolf-dog is racing towards me across the mud, tail waving like a flag. I don't understand. It can't really be happening, but it is, and my heart hammers so hard you can probably see it through my T-shirt. Cat screams and the big black-and-white lurcher dog launches herself at me, licking my face, twisting and yelping.

'What is this?' Cat is asking, but I'm down on my knees on the concrete, the big skinny dog dancing around me. Suddenly, out of nowhere, Lucky jumps in between us, yelping, grinning, not wanting to be left out. I can see Mum in the distance, grinning, and I scoop Lucky up, hold him tight.

'Feeling better, huh?' I grin. Then I turn to the big, scruffy wolf-dog leaping around me, tail lashing.

'Leggit,' I whisper into her sticky-up fur. 'Hey, hey, Leggit! It's really you! How are you, girl? What took you so long?'

I introduce Leggit to Lucky, and the two dogs circle warily, sniffing, then take off at top speed towards the van, where Mum is standing with a young man and woman. They were just twelve and thirteen that long-gone summer, younger than I am now, but I'd know Finn and Dizzy anywhere.

They were my best friends that summer I was seven, along with Leggitt, of course. My dad let me down, kept his distance and finally ran out on me, but Finn and Dizzy were always there, no matter what. They cared. I thought I'd have them forever, but after the bonfire accident, the summer fell apart, social services stepped in and gradually we lost touch.

Finn is taller, broader now, with dark dreadlocks down past his shoulders, pulled back from his face with a headband. His eyes are blue-grey and his mouth curves up in the biggest grin I've ever seen. Beside him, Dizzy is wiping her eyes, running towards me, whirling me round and round in a tight, tight hug.

'Dizzy!' I choke out. 'Finn!'

'Mouse, pal,' Finn laughs. 'It's so good to see you! We couldn't believe it when we got your letter, after all that time . . .'

My letter? I shoot a sidelong glance at Cat, and she can't meet my eye. Her mouth twitches into a smile.

'It went to Dad's place, obviously,' Dizzy explains. 'They were on holiday, but he passed it on the minute he got back. I couldn't believe it. It was the best surprise ever!'

'Too right!' I grin, and Cat winks at me.

The girl who gave me a handful of stars has just given me back my best friends, and I can't even begin to take it all in.

'We were going to write, but there's so much to catch up on,' Finn is saying. 'It's my brother's birthday tomorrow – remember Niall? He lives in Kent now. We're heading down to see him, so we thought we'd drop in on you!'

'We just couldn't wait,' Dizzy chips in. 'We found the flat OK, but Magi said you were out . . .'

'We came down to the van,' Mum says. 'Not a good idea to leave it parked here unattended. A minute more and the kids'd have picked it clean.'

'This is my girlfriend, Cat,' I tell them. 'And my dog, Lucky.'

'Hi, Cat,' they say. 'Hi, Lucky.'

Everyone is smiling and talking at once, and Leggit and Lucky are skittering around, tails in the air. I have about a million questions, but I don't know where to start.

'Can you stay?' I ask. 'I mean, you don't have to be at Niall's until tomorrow, do you?'

'No,' Finn says. 'We can stay for a bit. If you'll have us, that is!'

'You're very welcome,' Mum says. 'I wouldn't

leave the van here overnight, though . . . it might not be safe.'

'No problem,' Finn tells her. 'We'll stay a while, then head on down to Kent. I promised Dizz a whistle-stop tour of London, so if you want to show us the big city . . .'

'What now?' I ask. 'In the dark?'

'Why not?' Dizzy says. 'It'll be pretty. You can be our tour guides!'

We pile into the camper-van, Mum, Cat, Lucky, Leggit and me, with Finn and Dizzy in the front. Finn fires the engine up, and the whole van shakes and roars like a demented tractor. I frown. 'It sounds exactly like . . .'

'. . . the patchwork van?' Dizzy finishes for me. 'It is. Finn painted it up. We still take it to the festivals, in the summer. We do storytelling workshops, so we get in free!'

I think of the new-look patchwork van struggling over rutted ground, parking up beside a river with tents and tepees all around. Music playing into the night, wood fires burning, children running wild, the way we did at festivals long ago. I can't help smiling.

'Where to first?' Finn wants to know, turning out of the estate and on to the main road. 'Any ideas?'

'A magical mystery tour, yeah?' Mum suggests. 'Take a left here . . .'

'OK,' Finn says. 'We're not fast, but we're reliable. Actually, we're not reliable either, but we do have tea-making facilities . . .'

'I can't believe how tall you are, Mouse,' Dizzy says over her shoulder. 'What are you now, fourteen?'

'Yup.'

'Still into BMX bikes and beaches and tree houses?'

I frown. 'Not exactly. I kind of went off the whole BMX thing after the bonfire, y'know? And I haven't seen many beaches or tree houses, lately.'

'He's more into painting, these days,' Cat says. 'And stars.'

'Stars?' Dizzy asks. 'Remember when we used to look for the Pole Star, that summer? I still think of you, whenever I see it.'

I want to say that I think of her too, and Finn, Leggit, Tess and a half-dozen other people from that long-gone summer. I just grin at Dizzy through the darkened van, and she grins back, and I think she gets the message.

'What about your mum, Finn?' I ask. 'Is she still at Bramble Cottage?'

'Yeah, Tess is still there,' he says. 'And Gran. If you ever want a country holiday, you'd be welcome, Mouse — and you, of course, Magi, and Cat.

London's cool, but if you fancy a bit of peace and quiet . . .'

Finn takes care not to make the offer sound like charity, and Mum smiles in the darkness. She looks happy tonight, like the kind of person who might go for a holiday in the country. I think about the tree house with its roof of stars at Bramble Cottage, and about the veggie garden, the goat, the chickens. I refuse to think about the bonfire, or the BMX, or any of the stuff that happened afterwards.

'Take a right turn just here,' Mum instructs. 'Oxford Circus!'

We rumble past the famous shopping street, grinning at the flashing Christmas lights, the tacky neon Santas. 'Good job none of it's open,' Dizzy says. 'I haven't started my Christmas shopping yet!'

A few minutes later, we're heading for Trafalgar Square, where the giant Christmas tree glints and sparkles in the darkness.

'So, were you, like, childhood sweethearts?' Cat asks Finn and Dizzy. 'I didn't realize. Cool!'

'We weren't together the whole time,' Dizzy says.

'No, she ditched me in Year Nine,' Finn says. 'For some geek who helped her with her chemistry homework –'

'He was not a geek!'

'She got an A in her GCSE and dumped him the next day,' Finn tells us. 'Poor guy.'

'So you got back together?'

'Eventually. I turned up on the doorstep just before her seventeenth birthday in this old crate, and whisked her away to Glastonbury Festival. Haven't been able to shake her off since!'

Dizzy elbows him in the ribs. 'He's been plaguing me, more like,' she says. 'He got a place at music college in Birmingham, so there was no getting rid of him . . .'

'We share a flat now,' Finn says. 'It's a nightmare, but hey . . .'

We drive on through the night, rattling past Big Ben and the Houses of Parliament, talking non-stop, then head for Tower Bridge and the river. Finn parks down by the Thames Embankment, under the strings of fairy lights. This is the place Cat and I walked hand-in-hand after our posh tea in The Savoy, where we caught a river boat and then went on the London Eye. Now, the Eye is still, and the dark ribbon of water glitters with reflected light. A pale sliver of moon hangs above it, a perfect crescent in the dark sky.

'New moon,' Finn comments. 'We should all make a wish.'

But for once in my life, I've got pretty much everything I need. Mum is on one side of me, Cat on the other, Lucky curled up safely on my lap. Leggit, the big skinny wolf-dog, is stretched out at my feet, and Finn and Dizzy are telling me all about the festivals I've missed this summer. Who needs wishes?

Cat yawns. 'Tired?' Mum asks her. 'We can drop you off on the way back. It's a bit late.'

'I've got a key,' she replies sleepily. 'No problem.'

'We'll get moving,' Finn says. 'We can drive on down to Kent, be at Niall's by morning. But now we know where you are . . . well, we'll be seeing a lot more of you. That's a promise.'

Finn starts up the engine and we chug away into the night traffic, a deep blue, starry VW van on its way down to Kent via the Eden Estate. Cat's fallen asleep on my shoulder, her hair brushing my cheek, and Dizzy is telling me that her dad finally got married to his girlfriend, and that she has two new half-sisters. 'Weird, huh?' she says. 'Katie's four, Stella's six.'

We drop Cat at her gate, and I see a curtain twitch as she slides her key into the lock and waves goodnight. I hope she's not going to be in trouble. Finn drives on, finally turning into the Eden Estate. It's quiet, except for a gang of young men in hoodies lurking near Skylark Rise. One of them chucks a stone at the van, and it clatters against the side door.

'Tough place,' Finn comments. 'Don't think they like the van.'

'They don't like anything, that lot,' Mum says darkly. 'But like it or not, this place is changing. It's been sick and ugly and sad, a place where bullies rule and everyone else has to keep their head down. Not any more. People here are sick of being victims – they're learning to fight back.'

We pull up outside Nightingale House, spilling out on to the cracked concrete. Everyone hugs, and I hang on to Leggit for a long time. 'Sure you don't want to leave her?' I ask.

'Not this time,' Finn laughs.

'Good luck,' Dizzy says to Mum. 'With the Phoenix, with all of it, really. I think you're right – you can change things, if you try.'

Then she turns to me, handing me a Mars bar wrapped in star-printed paper. 'Take care, Mouse,' she says. 'Keep in touch. We'll see you soon!'

'Do you ever hear from Storm?' I make myself ask, just as Dizzy turns to jump back up into the cab.

Her face clouds. 'Sometimes,' she says. 'Birthdays, usually. She split with Zak, but you probably know that already . . .'

'No,' I whisper. 'No, I didn't. Is he . . . I mean, what . . .'

'He's still in India, the last I heard,' Dizzy says

softly. 'Scratching a living, hanging out on the beach, getting wasted. Different girlfriend every week, Storm says. You know Zak.'

But I don't, of course. I never did.

The icicle lights shimmer softly as we walk into the lobby of Nightingale House. Lucky starts to whimper. I hold him tighter, glancing around, but the place is deserted. 'Shhh,' I tell him. 'You're tired and it's late and you've had the worst week ever, but everything's fine now, Lucky. Seriously.'

But Lucky knows better than me, because when we step out of the lift on floor nine, it's clear that things are not fine. Things are not fine at all.

Two guys in overalls are trying to patch up what was once our front door. They have patched the shattered glass with board, smoothed the splintered wood. They are replacing the locks.

'No,' Mum says. 'Oh, no.'

A uniformed policeman walks towards us. 'Magi Kavanagh? Martin?' he asks. 'I'm afraid there's been some trouble. A break-in. Some damage . . .'

Mrs S. opens her door and peeps round it, wrapped in a pink dressing gown, her grey hair sticking up in wisps. 'Oh, Magi,' she says sadly. 'Mouse.'

She pulls the door wide and opens her arms, and Mum goes to her. They hug for a long moment, and when they pull apart, both are crying. 'Magi,' Mrs S. whispers. 'I'm so, so sorry. I heard all the commotion, about eleven o'clock it was, but I was scared to go out. I rang the police.'

Mum just nods, shakily.

'You might want to stay somewhere else tonight,' the policeman says gently. 'There's nothing you can do here right now.'

'Please,' Mrs S. urges. 'Stay here. If there's anything at all I can do . . .'

Mum just shakes her head. She squeezes the old lady's hand and steps round the policeman, pulling aside the crime-scene tape. We walk into the flat – what used to be the flat. It's like stepping into a nightmare. The cooker and the washing machine have been torn from the wall and smashed to pieces, and every piece of crockery we have has been broken. Someone has made a pile of the bedding, the curtains, the beanbags, then poured black paint all over them. The bathroom, the hallway and the scratchy nylon carpet have all been splattered too.

On the living-room wall, a single word has been daubed – *stupid*.

We were that, all right, to think we could go against Frank Scully.

'He must be back,' I whisper. 'And he knows about Lucky.'

'Guess so,' Mum says.

What would have happened if we'd been at the flat? Or if we'd gone out with Finn and Dizzy, leaving Lucky alone to recover from the kidnap? I shudder.

'It may just be an act of random vandalism,' the policeman is saying. 'Unless you know of anyone who may have a grudge against you?' Mum looks over her shoulder, but Mrs S. has retreated back to her flat.

'I'm standing witness against a man called Frank Scully in a month's time,' she says softly. 'He's a drug dealer, out on bail. I'm the only witness he hasn't scared off yet. I think he might just have a grudge, Officer.'

'Ah,' the policeman says, scribbling notes. 'That puts a very different spin on things. We'll make some enquiries. Once the boys there have made the flat safe for you, we'll go – we have everything we need for now. We'll call back around midday tomorrow, but I'd advise you both to find somewhere else to spend the night. You can't stay here.'

'It's our home,' Mum says, but the words come out as a sob. 'We're staying.'

The officer shrugs, shaking his head. The overalled guys are packing up now, checking the new lock, handing over a set of keys.

'You're sure?' the policeman asks. 'We'd really advise –'

'Sure,' Mum says. She steers the policeman into the corridor and closes the battered door firmly, taking a deep, raggedy breath. 'Oh, Mouse,' she says.

There isn't a bit of the flat that hasn't been trashed and ruined, that isn't wet with paint or glittering with broken glass.

'Where are the plants?' Mum wants to know. 'My plants!' But the big jungly plants that reached to the ceiling are gone, along with our TV, our toaster, our clothes. Mum picks up the telephone, a mess of wires and shattered plastic, then lets it fall again.

'I can't withdraw my statement, Mouse,' Mum says.

'I can't give Lucky back.'

Mum sinks down into a corner, leaning up against the wall, and I sit beside her, scooping Lucky on to my knee. 'Do you think this is the end of it?' I ask in a small voice. 'Or just the start?'

'I don't know,' Mum says.

I wake to a hammering on the door, and open my eyes to chaos. The flat looks worse in daylight, if that's possible. 'Mouse!' a familiar voice is yelling. 'Magi! Open up. It's me, Jake!'

I stumble to the patched-up door, open it a crack.

'Mouse,' Jake says. 'I heard. What can I do?'

'You can't do anything,' I say. 'Nobody can.'

I let the door swing wide, and Jake comes in. His eyes skim over the wreckage, registering shock, disgust, anger. He goes to Mum and hugs her lightly, as if she's something fragile that might break easily. Maybe she is.

'I had a visit last night from Frank Scully,' Jake says. 'He'd found out about Lucky. I acted dumb, pretended I knew nothing. I had to show him that I still had the key, swear black and blue I knew nothing about it. Don't know if he believed me.'

Mum narrows her eyes. 'You helped Mouse get Lucky back?' she asks.

'I had to,' Jake says, shoulders sagging. 'The dog was suffering.'

Mum looks at Jake with a new respect.

'Anyway, Scully took off in a real rage,' Jake goes on. 'I tried to phone you, but there was no reply. Then I heard the police cars, saw the plants –'

'The plants?' Mum echoes.

Jake takes her elbow and steers her out on to the balcony. The three of us look down on to the cracked concrete courtyard, now strewn with mangled plants, smashed pots, cushions, clothes, bits and pieces of our lives chucked out like so much rubbish.

'I wanted to warn you,' Jake says sadly. 'I just wasn't quick enough.'

'Doesn't matter,' I say. 'It wasn't your fault.'

There's another knock on the door, and Jake goes to open it. This time it's Mrs S. with a tray of tea and toast. 'Oh, my,' she says, eyeing the mess. 'This is going to take some cleaning up. I'd best get my mop bucket.'

'No, really, we can manage,' Mum argues as the old lady bustles away, but Jake just hands her a mug of tea and a slice of toast and tells her not to worry.

'Everyone needs help sometimes,' he says. 'Wouldn't you chip in, if you saw this happen to someone else?' He starts lifting the paint-spattered bedding out on to the balcony. When he has a big pile of it, he heaves it over and the whole lot crashes down on to the concrete below. 'I'll get a skip,' he tells me.

Mrs S. reappears with a fresh apron, a mop, a broom and a whole range of cleaning materials, just as Fitz and Chan appear with their mums. 'Jake said you might need a hand,' Fitz says. 'Man, what a war zone!'

Luke and Julie arrive next, along with a couple

of the Phoenix regulars who've heard and want to help. News travels fast on the Eden Estate, and by mid morning we have more offers of help than we know what to do with. Luke brings a wheelbarrow, and pushes barrowloads of trashed and ruined stuff along to the lift and down to the skip that Jake has organized. The paint-spattered carpet is rolled up and hauled away, bin bag after bin bag filled with rubbish. Slowly, bit by bit, we strip the flat.

Chan's mum rings around on her mobile for dustpans, brooms and mops, and a squad of helpers cleans up the broken glass, the splinters of wood. Mrs S. wipes the walls with soapy water and bleach, and even Fitz grabs a scourer and gets stuck in. At midday, the police arrive again, and Jake touches my elbow lightly.

'Time I was out of here,' he says.

'Thanks, Jake, for all this,' I say.

'Don't thank me,' he says with a shrug. 'Looks like you have a lot of friends.' He winks at me and slips quietly away.

The flat is chaos, with maybe a dozen people scrubbing, wiping, clearing. My CD player is lying down on the concrete courtyard in a dozen little pieces, but Fitz has his own player plugged in, pumping out a lively techno beat to keep everyone working hard. Someone has brought a large can of white emulsion paint, and Julie makes a start on painting out the *stupid* taunt.

'Is there somewhere we can talk?' one of the police officers asks.

Mrs S. invites us along to her flat. She bustles into the kitchen to make tea, and I can't help noticing that the table is still set the way it was on Friday, the same sponge cake wrapped in cling film, looking a little crispy now. Some of the hundreds and thousands sprinkled across the cupcakes have bled into the icing, the colours running like watercolour paint in the rain. Scully hasn't been round to see his gran yet – well, I guess he's had better things to do.

'We've spoken to Frank Scully,' the policeman says, and Mrs S., emerging from the kitchen with a laden tray, flinches at the mention of her grandson's name. The policeman, clearly, has no idea that she's anything to do with Frank. 'I'm afraid he has an alibi,' the policeman explains.

'Surprise, surprise.'

'He was in Luton at the time of the break in,' the policeman explains. 'We know he's been in the area, and a number of witnesses have confirmed that he was with them, at a nightclub, at the time of the disturbance. I'm sorry.'

'Me too,' I say.

'So . . . what happens now?' Mum asks.

The policeman shakes his head. 'We have no prints, no proof, no eyewitness accounts,' he says. 'Frank Scully has a watertight alibi. Unless something new turns up, there's very little we can do.'

Mrs S. is pouring tea into pretty china cups, but her hands shake and she puts the teapot down. 'It's not right,' she says in a quavery voice. 'What happened to Magi and Mouse is criminal, but my Frank wouldn't – he just couldn't . . .'

Mum runs a hand through her hair, embarrassed. 'It's OK, Mrs S., Frank has an alibi. He wasn't here last night, so of course, it couldn't have been him.'

'No,' Mrs S. says.

The policeman takes a sip of his tea, then stands, smiling sadly. 'Well,' he says. 'That's it, really. I'm sorry we haven't come up with anything more conclusive. Mrs Kavanagh – it's great to see the community rallying round to help you, but I have to advise you that whoever did this may still be out there. I don't want to alarm you, but . . . well, just be careful. OK?'

The policeman turns to go.

'Wait,' Mrs S. says into the silence. 'I don't think . . . I mean . . .'

The policeman puts a hand on her arm, reassuringly. 'I'm sure there's really no cause for concern,' he says.

'My Frank wouldn't do something like that,' she repeats. 'I'm sure he wouldn't. But . . . well, he's not telling you the truth, Officer, about where he was last night. He was here, on the estate.'

'What?' the policeman says. 'You saw him?'

Mrs S. sinks down on to a chair, and Mum goes to her, slipping an arm round her shoulder.

'I called the police, you know,' Mrs S. is saying. 'I heard all the racket, and I was frightened, of course, but things went quiet and I looked out into the corridor . . . about eleven, it was. I saw Frank, running down towards the lift. As I say, he wouldn't do a thing like that, but perhaps . . . perhaps he saw someone himself?'

The old lady looks confused, her face crumpled and sad. 'I just don't understand why he'd lie about it, that's all,' she says.

The policeman looks at Mrs S. for a long time. 'Are you sure?' he asks, gently. 'Are you sure the man you saw running towards the lift was Frank Scully? Could you have been mistaken?'

Mrs S. shakes her head. 'He's my grandson,' she says. 'Of course I'm sure.'

The policeman smiles and opens his notebook at a fresh page. 'I think,' he says briskly, 'we've just got ourselves an eyewitness account.'

By nightfall, the flat is looking less like the aftermath of a small hurricane and more like a place to live again. The walls have been painted white, a green nylon carpet has been rolled out across the living-room floor and new mattresses and bedding have been delivered, courtesy of Luke and Julie.

Cat, with a paintbrush in her hand and spatters of white emulsion in her hair, has been around all afternoon – Fitz rang her at lunchtime. 'It's awful,' she whispered into my hair when I first opened the door to her. 'Awful, awful, awful. Scully can't get away with it this time.'

'No,' I said, thinking of Mrs S. with her crumpled face and her pretty china teacups and her iced cakes going stale under a layer of cling film. 'This time, I don't think he can.'

Scully was taken into custody a few hours ago, once Mrs S. had given a formal police statement. I could see Mum taking in deep breaths of air as the police car drove away. Her shoulders relaxed, and the fear and anxiety slipped away from her face, her eyes. 'It's going to be OK,' she told me.

Maybe, just maybe, it is. Psycho Sam, the Rottweiler man, turns up while the clear-up crew are eating fish and chips, and promises he'll cut us a great deal on a new bathroom suite and get it installed next day.

'We'll all chip in,' Julie says. 'Right?'

'Right,' Chan's mum agrees. 'No arguments.'

Mum just shakes her head and shrugs, helplessly, and I know she's feeling the same way I do, overwhelmed with the support and help our friends and neighbours have given us today. I never really felt like I had a family before – it was always Mum and me, against the world. Now I can see that family comes in all shapes and forms. It's like a whole new constellation just appeared on my star map, and together we can tackle anything – even Scully.

There's a banging on the door, and Jake staggers into the flat carrying a six-foot potted palm. Behind him, a delivery guy from the local garden centre lugs in a Swiss cheese plant, almost as big.

'Jake!' Mum gasps. 'You shouldn't have! Oh . . .'

The tears that have been held back all day bubble up to the surface, misting her grey eyes. Jake just grins sheepishly, ruffling my hair, grinning. 'They're just plants,' he says.

To Mum, of course, they are much more than that.

People start drifting off, promising they'll be back next day if anything still needs doing. 'No, no,' Mum assures them. 'We can manage now. We'll be OK.'

I think maybe we will.

Of course, Psycho Sam collars Fitz and Chan for dog-walking duty, so Cat and I tag along for company. We leave Lucky with Mum, Jake and the garden centre man, sipping coffee made with a second-hand kettle, out of brand-new Woolworths mugs.

We head down to the first floor to collect the dogs. 'Here they are,' Psycho Sam says, handing them over. 'Be good, Jordan. Be good, Jade!'

'Jordan?' Cat echoes as we sprint after Fitz and Chan, who are now being towed rapidly along towards the lift. 'Jade? Sam's a big softy, isn't he? I bet these dogs wouldn't hurt a fly.'

'Dunno,' I say, seriously. 'Sam lives next door to a drug dealer. I suppose he reckons the dogs are good security.'

Cat blinks.

'He lives next door to a *dealer*?' she repeats. She stops short, staring back along the corridor, open-mouthed.

'Don't,' I hiss, dragging her towards the lift. 'It's no big thing. Everyone knows.'

'Everyone knows?' she asks, horrified. 'Everyone knows, and yet they don't *do* anything?'

I bundle Cat into the lift. 'What can we do?' Fitz asks, reasonably. 'The Eden Estate is full of dealers. You learn to live with it.'

'But those losers are the people who got Scully into drugs,' Cat says. 'They're his friends, right? They wreck lives. They probably helped to torch the Phoenix. And you guys are OK with all that?'

Jordan and Jade lurch out across the lobby, beneath the icicle lights. They bound out across the floodlit courtyard. 'We're not OK with it, obviously,' I say. 'Fitz is just saying, that's the way things are around here. You get to know stuff.'

'Up on the tenth floor, there are two flats next to each other where a couple of dealers live,' Chan tells Cat. 'Scully's in Eagle Heights, next floor down from me. There are dealers in every block.'

'You know where they live?' she asks, incredulous. 'All of them?'

'Not all,' Chan admits. 'Some, though.'

'Shut it, Chan,' I snap, and he shrugs.

'Just saying.'

It's cold, and the first real frost of the year has blackened and shrivelled the last of the flowers poking up through the ash and wreckage.

'Why won't the police do something?' Cat wails. 'It's crazy! It's wrong!'

'You need proof, man,' Fitz says. 'Nobody wants to point the finger.'

'Well, Mrs S. did,' Cat reminds us. 'She's probably the bravest person around here! If we could get a list together of where the other dealers are . . . mark them, somehow . . .'

'No,' I tell her.

'Bad idea,' Fitz chimes in. 'Haven't you had enough of trouble?'

Sometimes, though, I think that's the one thing Cat will never get enough of. She tugs at my arm, pulling me back as the dogs drag Fitz and Chan out of earshot.

'Mouse, listen!' she whispers, her eyes gleaming. 'If we could just find out who all the dealers are . . .'

'We could,' I say. 'But what's the point? We couldn't go to the police – they'd need proof, and we don't have that. Besides, it would be dangerous, and like Fitz says, we can't risk more trouble. It's not an option.'

Cat narrows her eyes. 'Not the police,' she says, slowly. 'I've got a better idea . . .'

Cat can wrap the world round her little finger. Before long, she's got me convinced that her crazy plan is worth one last risk, one last effort.

'You have to stand up for what you believe in,' she tells me. 'You can't stand by and let bad things happen without trying to stop them.'

I think of Mrs S., who stood up for what she believed in, even though it meant sending her grandson back to prison. The old lady looks crushed, beaten, lately, as if all the hope has been taken away from her. I suppose nobody ever said that doing the right thing was meant to be easy.

'People are learning to fight back around here,' Cat points out. 'They're angry about the Phoenix, they're fed up with being pushed around. Look at what's happening – the lobbies, the lifts, the flowers people have planted.'

'I suppose,' I say, doubtfully.

'We're not going to the police,' Cat promises. 'We're just going to make sure people know exactly who and where the dealers are. We'll shame them, right?'

I'm not convinced. I don't think the dealers have any shame.

'It's too dangerous,' I tell Cat. 'If we get caught –'

'We won't get caught,' Cat says.

It takes us two days to gather a list of the dealers on the Eden Estate. We talk to Fitz and Chan again, picking their brains without letting them know what we're planning. 'The less people know, the safer it'll be,' Cat says, but what we're doing is not safe, no matter how I look at it. We've just got one local thug off our case, and now Cat wants to stir up trouble with a whole bunch more? Bad news.

There are nine addresses, scattered across each of the four high-rise blocks. 'Just nine?' Cat demands. 'I thought there'd be more.'

It doesn't sound so many, but those nine people and their lackeys are responsible for a whole lot of misery, fear and pain. 'Nine,' I tell her. 'Fitz thinks the new blokes along the hall from his place are dodgy, but he's got no real evidence. They've been hanging around, getting pally with some of the dealers, but I think most likely they're just buying stuff.'

'We'll stick to the known dealers,' Cat says. 'We can't afford mistakes.'

I think that this whole idea is a mistake, but I swallow my fear and do my best to make sure nothing will go wrong. We plan our hit for Thursday night, when Mum, Luke and Julie are travelling to Liverpool to spend the following day checking out the anti-drugs charity working alongside the council up there. 'They're getting fantastic results,' Mum explains. 'We can learn so much from them, for when the Phoenix is back on its feet. Things are going to be different here, Mouse, I know they are.'

'When will you be back?'

'Friday night,' Mum says. 'Look, Mouse, I know Scully's safely out of the way again, but still, I don't like leaving you alone, not the way things are right now. Can you and Lucky stay with Fitz?'

'Maybe,' I bluff.

'D'you want me to call his mum, check it's OK with her?'

'No, no, I'll sort it,' I say. 'No hassle.'

Mum has learnt to live with the occasional graffiti hit, but I don't think she'd be as understanding if she knew what we're planning this time. It's better that she doesn't know.

'Don't do anything I wouldn't do,' she says before she goes.

'That gives me a pretty free rein,' I quip.

'Cheeky,' she laughs. 'Seriously, though. Take care of yourself.'

'I will. Don't worry, Mum. And good luck in Liverpool!'

Everything is ready.

It's four twenty-five in the early hours of Friday morning. Cat's parents think she's at Aditi's house, curled up in her *Hello Kitty* nightdress, spark out after a night of French revision and popcorn. Mum thinks I'm at Fitz's place, tucked up in the spare bunk with Lucky at my feet.

They're all wrong. Cat is dressed in an old jumper and ragged jeans, face disguised by a black fleece ski-mask with just a slit for the eyes and mouth. I pull on a black beanie and wrap a scarf round my mouth and nose, but I know that if we are seen, a scarf and a ski-mask won't save our skin.

'Scary,' I tell Cat, and she pulls the ski-mask off, grinning.

Lucky licks his lips and starts to whine. 'Be good, Lucky,' I say in a muffled voice, wondering how he can manage to look worried and disapproving at the same time. 'Don't wait up for us.'

Cat hugs me quickly in the darkness. 'Let's go.'

My heart is racing as we creep along the corridor, ride down in the turquoise tinselled lift and skulk across the courtyard. The estate is deserted and still. My senses are sharp with the adrenaline, but there's a heavy dread in my belly that feels like real fear. If I was the kind of boy who prayed, I'd be praying now, but the best I can do is look skywards, searching for stars. A bright, blinking light falls slowly through the darkness.

'Look,' I whisper to Cat. 'Shooting star! That's good luck.'

She rolls her eyes. 'It's a plane, you idiot,' she says, and when I look again I can see that she's right. Typical.

We start in Skylark Rise, on the seventh floor. Cat pulls on her ski-mask as we leave the lift. The corridor is empty, each scratched and ancient front door hiding nothing but silence. We linger outside number 83, uncertain, and then Cat hisses, 'Go!'

I start to spray, a quick blast of red that blooms like a flower against the dull, grey paintwork and drips down like blood. I step back and Cat uncaps her spray can, painting the words *dealers out* in spiky black letters. Before the paint has even begun to dry, we are back inside the lift, spray cans hidden, hearts hammering.

'One down, eight to go,' I tell Cat.

The second hit, down on the third floor, is just as smooth. Nobody sees us, and within minutes we're back in the lift, clunking slowly downwards. We come out through the lobby, cross towards Raven's Crest, and Cat elbows me in the ribs.

'Look!' she whispers. 'In the playground! They weren't there, before.'

Under the thin orange lamplight, two men are sitting on the battered roundabout, smoking and talking in low voices. The tips of their cigarettes glow red in the darkness. We tug off the scarf and the ski-mask, try to look casual.

'They're not interested in us,' I say, hoping I'm right.

Cat links my arm and we move out of view, into the lobby of Raven's Crest. The third graffiti hit goes without a hitch, and then we move on to the tenth floor. I've just sprayed my burst of red when a door opens along the corridor. 'What d'you want?' a voice asks.

Somehow, I drag up the name of the dealer who lives here. 'Looking for Carlo,' I answer. 'Seen him?'

'Don't you know what time it is?' the voice snaps back. 'People are trying to sleep! Clear off!'

The door slams, Cat sprays her *dealers out* slogan and we're off at a sprint. 'Close one,' Cat says, in the relative safety of the lift.

'Four down,' I whisper. 'Five to go.'

As we cross towards Eagle Heights, I see the figures in the playground, quiet now, still smoking. They make me feel faintly uneasy, as if they're watching us. Inside, there's a party going on at one of our target flats. Loud music booms out along the corridor, and it takes every bit of courage we have to walk towards that noise, but I spray my blood-red mark and Cat scrawls her message, and we're out of there. The next hit is easy by comparison, and now there are only three doors left to mark, all of them in Nightingale House.

'Almost there,' I say, as we come out of Eagle Heights, but straight away my scalp prickles and I look around me. I can smell trouble – something is going on. A couple of dark vans are parked across the way at Skylark Rise, two more down by Nightingale House. As I watch, another dark van slides into the road and turns down towards Raven's Crest.

'Weird,' says Cat.

The men from the playground are watching us, their faces moon-pale in the darkness. 'Kids,' one shouts across to us, his voice steely-cold. 'Go home. You hear me? Get out of here.'

We keep walking, heads down. 'You hear?' he repeats, falling into step behind us, and suddenly I feel cold all over. 'Go home.'

'OK, OK,' I say, trying to keep the fear from my voice. 'We're going.'

We make it to the lift in Nightingale House, wide-eyed. 'What was all that about?' Cat wants to know. 'Something dodgy, I bet.'

'Too right,' I say. 'Let's get this over with, yeah?'

On the tenth floor, our targets are side by side, two smartly painted doors. It should be fast, it should be easy, but my hand shakes as I start on the second door, and my scalp is still prickling with fear. I want to get out of here. I want to get out of here now. 'Cat,' I hiss. 'Leave it.'

Her green eyes blink, astonished, through the slit in her ski-mask. She shakes the spray can. 'Leave it? We're almost there!' she argues.

Suddenly, the lift clanks open at the end of the corridor and a whole bunch of men and dogs come charging towards us. Cat drops the spray can. I grab her arm and try to run the other way, but at the end of the corridor the fire-escape door bursts open and we're just about flattened in the stampede.

'Grab those damn kids!' someone yells.

Someone grabs my hood and yanks me to one side as the half-tagged doors splinter and give way. Men shove their way into the flats, uniformed men with bulletproof vests and guns. Policemen.

'Whoa,' Cat says from under her ski-mask. 'It's a raid!'

'Shut up,' a policeman snarls in her ear, and for once she does. A barrage of screaming, swearing and scuffling erupts from inside the flats, and I feel sick with fear.

A tall, sandy-haired man with breath that smells of cigarettes appears in front of us. 'I thought I told you kids to go home?' he says in that same ice-cold voice I recognize from earlier. 'Now look what's happened. You've got yourselves mixed up in something you really don't want to be mixed up in.'

'We'll go home now,' I squeak. 'Promise.'

The plain-clothes policeman sighs. 'Too late for that,' he says. 'Graffiti vandals, aren't you? And playing a very dangerous game, if you're doing what I think you were doing. I think we'd better take you along to the station, get your parents in.'

Cat pulls her ski-mask off, revealing golden-brown corkscrew hair and wide, anxious eyes. 'Noooo . . .' she says. 'Please. Can't you let us go? This was a mistake, a stupid mistake.'

The policeman raises one eyebrow. 'It's that all right, miss,' he says. 'Boys, take them down to the car.'

29

Two policemen walk us down to one of several squad cars that have joined the black vans outside Nightingale House. As we emerge into the cold night air, Cat wriggles and ducks and tries to make a break for it, but the policeman holds her firm.

'You're goin' nowhere, miss,' he says. 'Except for the station.'

As we are driven through the Eden Estate, it's clear that we've chosen the worst of all possible nights for our hit. The police, who for weeks have seemed less than bothered by the estate's problems, have clearly been planning this raid for a while. Outside every high-rise block, the black vans have been joined by police vans and squad cars. Officers are watching each exit, talking into radios, coordinating everything. I wonder if they have the same nine addresses we had. I hope so.

At the police station, we get put in a bare little room with a sleepy policewoman for company. I've been in police stations a bunch of times. When I was a kid, with Mum, once with Dizzy and Finn that long-ago summer, and more recently, of course, for crimes against a bus stop in Islington.

After a long wait, the sandy-haired plain-clothes cop from the raid turns up. He eyes us, coldly.

'We need names and addresses,' he says. 'Get your parents in.'

'My mum's away,' I say. 'Won't be back till evening.'

He raises an eyebrow. 'Other relatives?'

'None.'

'You've been in trouble before,' he says to me, scanning a print-out in his hand. 'Vandalism. Graffiti damage is a serious offence, you know!'

'I know,' I sigh.

'You have a named social worker, David Thomas. I'll call social services, see if they can send someone out.'

'He'll be overjoyed,' I say. Cat squirms with discomfort, and I remember that Dave is her social worker too.

'It may not be him, personally,' the sandy-haired guy is saying. 'Not at this hour of the morning. They'll send someone, though. What about your parents, Catrin?'

'Please don't tell them,' Cat pleads. 'I'm so, so sorry. I promise –'

'We have no choice,' he snaps. 'You were caught

committing criminal damage outside the homes of two notorious drug dealers. Have you any idea at all how dangerous that could have been? You could have fouled up a police drugs raid that has taken us months to plan. It's a miracle you're still here to tell the tale.'

'We didn't know!' Cat says. 'We thought you didn't care about the dealers. You let that creep Scully out on bail, and look what happened!'

I think of Lucky, tied by his washing-line lead in the corner of the lock-up, and Mum, determined to speak out at Scully's trial. I still can't let myself imagine what might have happened if Scully had come calling when we were all at home. Sometimes, when you think nobody else cares, you take crazy risks, to make a point, to make a difference.

'We were only trying to help!' Cat appeals.

The sandy-haired guy shakes his head. 'Remind me to stay well clear the next time you kids decide to help anybody,' he says. 'You could have wrecked the whole operation. We've had plain-clothes officers on the estate for weeks now. We let Scully out on bail because we wanted him to lead us to his suppliers – we've had him tracked, the whole time. What happened to your flat, son, that was unfortunate – but we'd have nailed him for it, with or without his gran's statement.'

I open my mouth and close it again, speechless. The police let Scully out deliberately, so he could lead them to the drugs suppliers? All of the bad stuff that's happened over the last week or so could have been avoided. It's like it was all a game, and one we were never going to win.

'You knew?' Cat asks, frowning. 'You planned this, all the time?'

'And you kids almost blew it,' the policeman says. 'Still . . . you didn't, I guess. I'm going to let you off with a caution, but if I ever see either of you in this place again, I'll be down on you like a ton of bricks. Got that?'

'Yes, sir,' I say. 'Thank you, sir.'

'So. Catrin. Your parents, please.'

Cat bows her head and gives out her mum's name and address, and the policeman scribbles down the information and walks away, leaving us alone with the silent policewoman.

'I am in soooo much trouble!' Cat wails.

I shrug. 'Your parents won't be pleased, but they'll get over it,' I tell her. 'Admit it, Cat – wasn't there just a little bit of you that knew this might happen?'

'No!' she protests.

'Come on,' I argue. 'When you run as close to the wind as you do, you're gonna get caught sometime. They'll forgive you.'

'But you might not!' she bursts out. 'Omigod, I've ruined everything!'

'Cat, shhh,' I tell her. 'We're OK, aren't we? We've got off with a police caution. And it sounds like the raid was a success too, and that's brilliant news.'

'But –'

'No buts,' I tell her. I slip my arm round her and pull her close, and she leans against me, her head on my shoulder, her vanilla-scented hair soft against my cheek. That's how we are sitting half an hour later, when the door swings open again.

Cat's mum comes in, anxious and tired, her face a perfect mask of dismay. Her eyes lock on to mine. 'You!' she says. 'The boy from drama club!'

'Me,' I admit. 'About that whole drama club thing . . .'

But I can't explain, because before I get the chance, Dodgy Dave appears right next to Cat's mum, his hair sticking up in clumps as if he just rolled out of bed. Well, he probably did.

'Mouse,' he says. 'What the . . .?'

Cat's mum flings her arms round her, and then, to my horror, Dodgy Dave does the same. That's taking the whole social worker thing a little too far, I reckon. I take a step back, confused.

Dave puts an arm round Cat's mum, and that's even weirder. The super-keen white social worker and the sad-eyed black lawyer huddle together, like they belong. My head struggles to make sense of it all. Dave Thomas. Mia Thomas. Catrin Thomas.

'I'm sorry I lied,' Cat says huskily, and I realize she's looking at me. She turns back to the adults. 'To you too. We had a plan . . . and then . . .' She runs out of ideas and shakes her head silently, eyes bright with tears.

Dodgy Dave glares at me over his glasses. In all the years I've known him, I've never seen him look this angry. His hands are balled into fists, as if he'd like to punch me, and his voice trembles as he speaks.

'Mouse,' he says. 'Just what in hell have you done to my daughter?'

I'm not just confused, I'm numb. I don't understand what's going on, and nor does Dave, by the look of it. He looks at Cat, shakes his head. 'You've been hanging out with this – this delinquent?' he splutters. 'This loser?'

That hurts, coming from someone who is supposed to care about me. It hurts more than I would ever have imagined.

'Dad,' Cat says to Dave. 'Please!'

Dad? Dad? I look at Cat and her eyes slide away from mine, and I realize that she was right. Everything is ruined.

There's a whole lot of fuss and confusion before the police are ready to let us out of there. Dave manages to prove that he is my designated social worker as well as Cat's dad, and finally, after about a million warnings of what might happen if we're ever in trouble again, we are released into the thin, cold December morning.

Dave drives through the early morning traffic in

silence, Cat's mum stony-faced in the passenger seat. Cat reaches for my hand in the back seat of the car, but I pull away, my head a mess of anger and betrayal.

'You lied,' I hiss. 'All this time, you lied. You let me think Dave was your social worker, when all the time . . .'

'I'm sorry,' Cat says again, but the words sound empty, hollow.

'What was I, some kind of charity project?' I ask softly. 'Or were you just slumming it? Notching up some bad-girl kudos with your posh mates? Poor little rich girl, hanging out with the boy from the Eden Estate.'

She just turns her head away.

Back at the house, Dave marches us into the kitchen. 'We need to know what's been going on,' he says. 'Catrin was supposed to be spending the night with a friend. At six in the morning we get a call to say she's in police custody, after a graffiti attack on the homes of known drug dealers on the Eden Estate! She's just a kid, Mouse!'

'We're not kids,' I snap back, defiantly. 'We're fourteen.'

Dave looks at me for a long moment, his eyes weary. 'Fourteen?' he asks. 'Is that what she told you? Catrin is only twelve.'

Twelve? I sink down on to a wooden chair. Cat

won't meet my gaze. In her cheeks, two pink spots appear. 'If I'd told you I was twelve, you'd have treated me like a kid,' she says. 'You'd have seen me differently. Like if I'd told you that Dave was my dad.'

'Well, yeah,' I admit. 'Obviously.'

I'm seeing everything differently now. Twelve isn't old enough to stay out all night on graffiti hits, or to stay over at your boyfriend's place when your parents think you're at a mate's. Twelve-year-olds shouldn't skive school or steal chocolates, and they shouldn't kiss you the way Cat kisses me. Twelve? I rest my head in my hands.

'You didn't know?' Dave asks.

'No, I didn't know.'

'Even so,' he says. 'You must have seen that Catrin was an unhappy, vulnerable girl. You've latched on to her and dragged her down . . . she's been totally out of control, these last few weeks.'

'It wasn't like that,' Cat protests. 'Mouse helped me.'

'Helped you?' Mia Thomas bites out. 'Ha! He's helped you to skip school, flunk your tests, stay out all night doing lord knows what . . .'

'Two hundred quid went missing from my wallet a couple of months back,' Dave tells me. 'I couldn't believe it was Cat, but . . . well, it makes sense now, doesn't it? She's been hanging out on the Eden

Estate with you, spending it on drink and cigarettes and . . . and –'

'No!' I argue. 'Nothing like that, I promise. I wouldn't! I don't smoke, or drink . . . or anything else!'

'You want me to take the word of a boy who can't stay out of trouble for five minutes at a time?' Dave laughs. 'I know too much about you, Mouse. You're trouble. You always will be. Can't you see that?'

I hang my head.

'Dad, Mum, stop it!' Cat cuts in. 'Mouse is my friend. I don't care if you believe me or not, but he has helped me – he's taught me about right and wrong, about friendship, about love.'

'Love?' Dave just about chokes.

'He cares about me,' Cat ploughs on. 'He really, really cares, which is more than you two do.'

I look at Dave. His mouth is opening and closing slowly, like someone underwater. 'Catrin, that's not fair . . .' he says.

'No, it's not,' she snaps back. 'My life has never been fair, not since Josh.'

There's a silence, a long, painful silence. Like an idiot, I try to break it. 'Maybe things will be better now,' I say. 'Now that Josh is well again. Now that he's coming home.'

Dave's face pales, then flushes a slow, dark pink.

Mia Thomas blinks, and her face seems to collapse. She hides behinds her hands, sobbing quietly.

'Josh won't be coming home,' Dave says icily. 'He died, a year ago. Didn't she tell you?'

My stomach turns over. Everyone has a dark secret, Cat once told me. Something buried, hidden, something that gnaws away at them, messing up their head, eating at their happiness from inside. I thought I knew the secret, but it was just another lie.

Cat won't look at me. 'It's like our lives ended then too,' she says to her parents. 'We're all in mourning for a little boy who's never coming back. Never, OK? Don't you see that?'

'We've lost one child,' Mia whispers. 'We don't want to lose you.'

'You don't even notice I'm alive, half the time!' Cat flings back. 'You're so wrapped up in the past it takes something like this for you to see that I'm hurting too!'

'You've been lashing out for a year now!' Dave retaliates. 'We've tried to be patient. We've tried to be understanding –'

'Did you ever try just being there for me?'

'We're always there for you!'

'It doesn't feel like that.'

'Catrin, don't punish us for what happened to Josh,' Mia says. 'We loved him, but we couldn't make him better. Losing him has made you all the more precious to us, but you've been on a self-destruct mission for months . . .'

Cat takes a deep breath. 'I felt like I didn't matter,' she tells them. 'Then I met Mouse, and just for a little while, I didn't feel that way any more.'

Dave sighs, sinks down on to a chair. He looks broken and defeated.

I'd like to tell Dave it's OK, that it doesn't matter that he just called me a delinquent and a loser, but I can't. It matters. My head feels like it's filling up with smoke and lies, splitting in two.

Cat reaches over, touches my hand, but I flinch. I don't know what to think, what to feel. Should I feel sorry for her, or angry that she's lied to me for so long? It's like the last few weeks have been some elaborate game, designed to wind her parents up, catch their attention at last.

She's more messed up than I ever imagined. All the good times, all the special times we shared were based on lies. Did I ever know her at all?

'Cat and Mouse,' I say, coldly. 'That's a joke – and the joke was on me, right? Well, good one, Cat. You had me fooled. You know what, though? Next time you start playing games, remember that other people have feelings too. Other people get hurt.'

'Mouse, that's not the way it was!' she protests.

'That's the way it looked to me,' I say. 'You know what? Forget it. I hope things work out for you, OK?' As I walk away, I can hear Dave calling my name, Cat crying, Mia comforting her. I don't look back.

A cat-and-mouse game can only ever end in tears.

Mouse . . .

Don't walk out of my life. You're my best friend – more than my best friend, OK? I need you. I let you down and I lied, but I never meant to hurt you, I swear. It started off as a game, wanting to hang out with you – a cool way to wind my parents up. It didn't stay that way. Pretty soon, you were the only thing that mattered.

I messed up, big style. I didn't think you'd want to know if you sussed I was only twelve, or worked out that Dave was my dad. I was right too, I guess. Lying about Josh was different. I was trying to fool myself, really, make out that there could still be some kind of happy ending. Crazy, right? It's just that I loved Josh, and I think you'd have loved him too, and I so, soooo wanted things to be different.

Sometimes, the truth just hurts too much.

Dad said he handled things badly, said things he shouldn't have said. He won't be your social worker any more, anyhow – he's got a new job at a youth project up in Brixton, starting in January. Shorter hours, less stress. We're going to family counselling, which is kind of weird, but Dad says we all need some help to get over the hole that Josh left in our lives. Maybe he's right.

Mouse, I'm missing you like mad. Lucky too. Give him a hug for me, yeah? You were the best thing that ever happened to me, and I let you down, stuffed up, lost you. I guess I only have myself to blame. Dad says it's probably all for the best, because we come from different worlds, but I liked your world, Mouse. I liked *you*.

After Christmas, Dad's taking us away for a few weeks, a proper holiday, somewhere hot and sunny. He says that'll cheer me up, but I don't think anything will ever cheer me up again. I feel so sad.

Please get in touch, Mouse. Please?

Cat xxx

That was four weeks ago. I tore the letter into tiny pieces and let the pieces drift into the waste-paper bin like snow. I wasn't ready to get in touch, I wasn't ready to forgive or forget, or even to understand.

Mum knew something had gone wrong between me and Cat, but she also knew me well enough not to ask too much. 'Sometimes,' she told me,

'You just have to work things out on your own. Think it through.'

Maybe. Sometimes, though, it's easier not to think about things.

Things are changing on the Eden Estate – it's like the whole place can breathe at last. It said on TV that the police raid was one of the most successful ever – hundreds of thousands of pounds' worth of drugs were seized, and a dozen arrests were made on the Eden Estate alone. The bigshot suppliers Scully led the police to were arrested and charged too – the guys who pulled the strings, masterminded the whole business. They didn't live around here, of course. They had posh houses with swimming pools and triple garages filled with fancy cars, all bought with drugs money. These guys were running drugs all over the south of England.

I had to tell Mum how I got tangled up in it all, of course. If I hadn't, she'd have heard from the social services anyhow – I figured it was better coming from me.

'Oh, Mouse,' she said, her eyes wide. 'No way!'

The colour drained from her face, and she was trembling as she pulled me close. 'Of all the nights to go away. Promise me you won't try anything like that again – it was dangerous, Mouse, way too dangerous. No more risks, no more vandalism, no more graffiti.'

I blinked and chewed my lip and finally I promised, and I'll stick to it too. Mum needs me and I need her, and neither of us need any extra hassle. We've had enough of that to last a lifetime.

Scully's trial finally came up, and Mum stood as a witness just like she said she would. Mrs S. stuck by her statement too, and a few other locals came up with evidence that showed Frank Scully hadn't got everybody running scared. He would have faced a good long stretch inside, but you know what? The weasel turned traitor and grassed up his mates, giving evidence against the other Eden Estate dealers.

'He did the right thing in the end,' Mrs S. said. 'My Frank.'

Well, maybe. Maybe he just wanted a lighter sentence, though, and that's what he got, for cooperating with the police. Still, it was three years, so we won't be seeing him around for a while.

'I told him you'd be keeping Lucky,' Mrs S. said to me, after her first prison visit. 'He said that might be for the best.'

'Frank Scully said that?' I asked, amazed. 'Really?'

Mrs S. looked shifty. 'Perhaps not in those exact words,' she admitted. 'I told him, though, that it was time he grew up and took responsibilty for his mistakes. Lucky's better off with you – he knows that. He still listens to his old gran!'

So Lucky became our dog, officially, or as official as anything ever gets around here, and that was one good thing.

Eden won't ever be perfect, of course, but it's better, for sure. Work started on the new community buildings just before Christmas – council workers came in diggers to break up the concrete courtyard, map out the new community garden. Mum was involved from the start – she got the garden centre guy, the one who brought the Swiss cheese plant, to do some designs and donate some plants. Our flat looks like a high-rise greenhouse, these days. The balcony is stuffed with twiggy fruit trees and trays and trays of budding daffodils and primroses just waiting to be planted out.

Jake has been hanging around Mum, lately, making her laugh with cheesy chat-up lines and offers of fancy dates involving nightclubs, cocktails and flash cars. She's not interested. She's spending more and more time with the garden centre guy, talking about hardy perennials and compost heaps and the best varieties of lettuce.

'Women,' Jake sighed. 'They're a mystery, Mouse, mate – every one of them. I've never figured them out yet.'

It's not so hard to figure – Jake's still up to his

ears in dodgy car deals and iffy deliveries, and Mum's not crazy about that. She prefers the kind of date where she can stay out late planting hedging all round the perimeter of the new community garden.

Me, I got wrapped up in the Green Vale Comp mural. Mr Brown wanted something cultural and uplifting, a landscape or a pretty rural scene. I had other plans. I marched into his office on the first day of the January term with a folderful of designs that made his eyes open wide. 'Ah,' he said. 'Not what I was expecting, but . . . well, you're the expert, Kavanagh. I'll leave it to you, shall I?'

He looked terrified when I turned up the next day with a box full of spray cans, but I promised this would be my last graffiti hit ever. It took me weeks, working in school time and out of it. I painted giant swirls of red and yellow and turquoise, silver stars and orange spirals and curling fronds of emerald green. I added a trail of little cat footprints, weaving in and out of the patterns, and Fitz spotted them and raised an eyebrow, smirking.

'So you're over her, huh?' he said.

'Over who?' I asked.

Fitz just laughed. 'Man,' he said. 'You've got it bad.'

*

It doesn't matter whether I'm over Cat or not, though – by now, she'll be over me. She's had a chance to think, a chance to let go, a chance to move on. I had my chance, and I didn't respond, and now it's most likely too late. Who knows, maybe she's better off without me.

I walk Lucky through the estate, hands in pockets against the cold. A couple of flakes of white drift past my face, swirling around in the wind, and I shiver and tug my beanie hat lower.

Cat was trouble, I know. She lied to me, used me, played games with my head, but there was another side to her too. The money she took from her dad's wallet wasn't for drink or ciggies, it was to pay a vet's bill. She bought me neon stars, showed me real ones, stroked the tight, crumpled skin of my cheek and didn't flinch. She wrote a letter to friends from the past I thought I'd never see again, and brought them back into my life. Cat cared.

Flakes of snow are landing on my fringe, stinging my cheeks. Lucky tries to chase the flakes, snapping at them as they fall. It never snows in London, or hardly ever. It feels like magic, like tiny, perfect stars, falling all around. A smile tugs at my mouth, my heart, and even though it's cold I feel like I'm warming up, defrosting, after a long time of feeling numb.

The snow falls faster now, and I stop beside the

fenced-off building site, the abandoned diggers hunched in the darkness. I look up into the navy-blue sky, and I see the snowflakes falling softly, relentlessly out of the darkness.

Beyond the whirling snowflakes, way up above Nightingale House, I think I see a bright star, silver-white, glinting above me, and then it's gone, lost in the gathering storm.

By morning, the whole world is muffled and quiet.
The new garden is carpeted with snow, the diggers
draped in white. All the ugliness has gone, as if it
were never there at all. Lucky is smiling hopefully,
his tail beating against the floor.

It's very early, but I pull on a hat, a hoodie, a
jacket. I lace up my Converse trainers and slip out
of the flat, along the corridor to the lift. Down in
the lobby, everything is quiet beneath the twinkling
icicle lights, and outside the estate is still and
silent.

Lucky launches himself forward and almost
vanishes into a snowdrift. He emerges grinning, his
tail twitching. My trainers crunch into unspoilt
snow as if I am the only boy alive, and I walk
through the Eden Estate, catching snowflakes on
my tongue.

I try to imagine the place in a year's time. I
picture kids playing on a new, revamped playground,
mums chatting over their pushchairs outside the

239

nursery, oldies calling into the Day Centre for a cup of tea and a biscuit. The garden will be bursting with colour and life, and the new Phoenix will be up and running, and better than ever. It's hard to see the future, but snow has a way of washing the whole world clean, making anything seem possible.

Almost anything.

Seeing Cat again is going to be the hardest thing of all. I know I've let her down – I wasn't there for her when she needed me. I got angry, and I backed off and walked away. I tried to forget her, but I couldn't.

Some people are just part of your life, whether you like it or not.

There's my mum, who messed up so badly when I was a kid she almost didn't make it through. She did, though, and now her whole life is about helping others to survive, even when everyone else has given up on them.

There's my dad, who didn't really want to know me, but gave me my crooked teeth, my love of colour and countryside and risk-taking. As dads go, he's pretty useless, but who knows, one day I might just save my money and buy me a ticket to India and surprise him. Wonder what he'd say about that?

Bad stuff happens sometimes, and there's not a

whole lot of point in looking around for someone to blame it on. Who's to say my life would have been easier if Dad had been around? I used to think so, but now I'm not so sure. These days, I live my own life and I make my own luck, and that's something I think he'd understand. Besides, if Dad hadn't been so hopeless, I might never have found people like Finn and Jake. Even – don't laugh – Dodgy Dave and Mr Brown. There are plenty of people out there who care, or try to, if you just give them a chance.

Lucky – well, Lucky is my best friend. His lopsided grin, his pirate patch, his murky past . . . I didn't rescue him, he rescued me.

As for Cat, well, I realized a while ago that trust is something you either have or you don't have, no matter what. OK, so she lied to me. So what? I knew everything I needed to know about her anyway. I knew that she was messed-up and lost and lovely, and that all she ever wanted to do was to make the world a better place. She wanted to be loved too, and that's where I let her down.

I walked away from her, and nothing has been worth anything since then, nothing at all. I'm hoping it's not too late to tell her that.

I've left the Eden Estate behind me, and I'm cold now, my feet soaked and frozen as I trudge along the snow-caked pavements. The trees in Cat's road are bare, their branches bowed with snow, and when we get to her house I can see that it's still too early to call on her, way too early. The curtains are closed, the house still and silent.

I push the gate open softly, creating a mini-snowdrift. What if she doesn't want to see me? Four weeks have gone by since she wrote me that letter, and a lot can change in four weeks.

I don't know what I'd say to her, anyway – words have never been my strong point. When I don't know what to say, I say nothing at all. Lucky blinks up at me, tail wagging. I root through my rucksack and my fingers close round a can of paint, a half-used can of red. I take it out, shake it, and start to work.

I've never painted on snow before, but it can't be vandalism because the snow will be gone in a few days' time. That's what I reckon, anyhow. The red paint bleeds softly on to the crisp, white snow and pretty soon I step back and there is a giant heart curving across the snow-covered lawn beneath Cat's bedroom window. I tag a little mouse-face and a cheeky cat-face underneath it, then I whistle Lucky softly and we walk away, leaving two sets of perfect tracks in the snow.

Later on, I'm sitting on the corrugated roof of the bus stop along the road, eating a Mars bar, legs dangling. Lucky is tucked inside my jacket, a long-suffering expression on his face. My bum has frostbite and my legs are like blocks of ice, but I can't give up, I can't go home. Not yet.

An old lady comes along, looks up and bashes my feet with her walking stick. 'Bloomin' hooligan,' she says crossly.

A girl appears in the distance, a cool, cute, skinny girl with coffee-coloured skin, walking fast, slipping and sliding in the snow. She's wearing a little parka jacket with fur round the hood, corkscrew curls of golden-brown hair flying out around her face. Under the parka, I see what looks like a *Hello Kitty* nightdress over black leggings, and on her feet are red fluffy funfur slippers, which may explain why she's slithering around so much.

Lucky wriggles out from my jacket, tail wagging, his face one huge grin that stretches from ear to ear.

'Hey,' says the girl. She looks up at me with slanting green eyes that are wet with tears, starred with snowflakes.

'Hey,' I grin. 'What took you so long?'

Fabuloso EXCLUSIVE sneak preview
of Cathy's new novel . . . coming in
August 2008!

Ginger Snaps

Ginger Brown . . . it sounds like a colour on a paint chart, not a name. It sounds like a joke or a new shade of hair dye, or one of those treacly kind of cakes that nobody really likes. What sort of parents would call their kid something like that? Well, mine, obviously.

They didn't mean to ruin my life. They thought they were being quirky and cool and original, but actually they were working their way through the spice rack, taking inspiration from those little jars with funny names and even funnier ingredients. Seriously, if Dad hadn't been a curry fanatic it might never have happened.

They named my big sister Cassia, after a sort of aromatic tree bark you put in chicken korma, and me . . . well, they named me Ginger. If I didn't have hair the colour of grated carrots, I'd maybe be able to forgive them . . . but then again, maybe not.

With a name like Ginger, I didn't stand a chance.

*

I worked that out way back on the very first day of primary school when I told the teacher my name and saw her mouth twitch into a smirk. It was worse with the kids – they didn't just smirk, they laughed. The boys pulled my plaits and asked why my parents named me after my hair colour, and the girls asked if I thought I was one of the Spice Girls because they were still popular back then.

I went home after the first day and told Mum and Dad I wanted a different name, like Kerri or Emma or Sophie, and they just laughed and told me not to be silly. It was good to be different, they said, and Ginger was a beautiful name – unique, striking, unforgettable.

Well, it was that all right.

I never really knew what to say to the jokes and the teasing. 'Don't let it get to you,' Cass used to tell me. 'Just laugh it off or ignore it, OK?'

It was easy for her to say. She was in high school by then, cool and confident and always surrounded by friends. She had auburn hair too, but nobody ever seemed to call her names.

I worked out that the easiest way to avoid being teased was to keep my mouth shut, keep my head down and pretend I didn't care.

'She's very quiet,' Miss Kaseem told my parents at the start of Year Six. 'A lovely girl, but she doesn't join in with the others much. Not at all like Cassia was.'

I suppose I should be grateful Miss Kaseem didn't tell them the rest of it. How I never got picked for playground games, never had a partner for PE or project work, never got invited to sleepovers or parties or trips to the cinema with the other girls. I was an outsider, a loser. I tried to be invisible, sitting on my own in the lunch hall, eating an extra helping of apple pie and custard because it was something to do — a way to fill the time, a way to fill the hole inside me, the place where the loneliness was.

'Have you seen her?' I heard Chelsie Martin say to her friends one day. 'She's soooo fat! I saw her eat two packets of crisps at break, *and* she had an extra helping of chips at lunch. Gross!'

I just sat and smiled and pretended I hadn't heard, and when Chelsie had gone I ate a Twix I'd been saving for later, without even tasting it.

I thought it would go on like that forever.

Mum and Dad were anxious by then, always asking if I wanted to invite a friend over for tea, or go to dance classes like Cass or swimming club or karate. 'It'd be fun,' Mum would wheedle. 'You'd make lots of new friends, and get fit too . . .'

That's how I knew *they* thought I was fat too, as well as a loser. I wasn't the right kind of daughter. I wasn't the kind of girl who could make a name like Ginger seem cute and quirky.

When my eleventh birthday rolled around, Mum and Dad asked if I wanted a party. I said no, I was too old for that kind of thing.

'You're never too old for fun,' Dad had said, and I could see a flicker of something behind his gaze. Worry? Disappointment? 'You never have your friends around any more. What about a trip to the cinema, or the ice rink? Would that be grown-up enough for you?'

Sometimes you go along with something even though you know it's a bad, bad idea. 'What if nobody comes?' I'd said feebly to Cass, but she'd just laughed.

'Of course they'll come,' she'd said.

So we planned an afternoon at the ice rink, all expenses paid, followed by burger and chips in the cafe that looked over it. Mum had made a chocolate layer cake for afterwards with eleven little candles. I was excited, in spite of myself. Cass let me use some of her sparkly eyeshadow, and I wore my new pink minidress with the pop-art flowers and a new pair of jeans. I thought I looked good.

We'd arranged to meet outside the ice rink at two. Emily Croft and Meg Walters arrived dead on time. They were best friends; geeky, serious girls who sometimes let me hang out with them at break. 'Who else is coming?' they asked.

'Oh, everybody,' I told them, even though there

was already a little seed of doubt eating away at my heart. 'Chelsie and Jenna and Carly and Faye . . . everyone.'

I'd asked every girl in my class, because Cass said there was room for everyone at the ice rink and, even if they weren't all special mates, it would be a good chance to get to know them a bit more. I wanted to be the kind of girl who could invite a whole bunch of kids to her party. I didn't want to let her down. I asked everyone, and most people had said they'd be there.

So where were they? At half past two, Dad looked at his watch for the hundredth time and said maybe the others had got mixed up about the time. 'Cass, you take Ginger and the girls in,' he decided. 'Your mum and I can stay here for a bit, wait for the others. Perhaps they thought it was three?'

Emily Croft took a folded invitation from her pocket and looked at it. 'It says two,' she said, and I hated her for that. For not pretending that there was a mistake or a misprint or a traffic jam in town . . . Anything. Anything at all to take away the sick ache inside me.

Cass took Emily, Meg and me inside. I felt like I was holding myself together, as if the slightest knock might make me crumble. There was a stinging sensation behind my eyes. We handed in our shoes and pulled on ugly white boots with sharp silver blades, lacing them up tightly. Then we clomped across to the rink, wobbling slightly, and edged our way on to the ice. It was cold, and my feet felt like they would slip from under me at any moment.

At first all I could do was cling on to the edge, but Cass wasn't going to allow that of course. She took my hand and prised me away from the rail, and slowly, haltingly I took my first few steps on the ice. It *was* fun. Pretty soon the four of us were slithering about, grabbing on to each other and yelping with terror whenever anyone swooped past.

After a while, Cass spotted Mum and Dad watching from the sides, and skated over to talk to them, leaving Emily, Meg and me together. That's when I saw them – Chelsie, Jenna, Carly and Faye – just ahead of us on the ice.

My face lit up. They were here after all – Chelsie and the others, the four most popular girls in the class. It must have been a mix-up about the time, like Dad had said. I skated towards them with a grin a mile wide.

Chelsie spoke first. 'Hi, *Ginger*,' she said. Her voice sounded mean and smirky, the way it always did when she spoke to me. Then again, that wasn't exactly often. 'Thought we might see you here. Sorry we couldn't make your party . . . we had something better to do.'

Chelsie and the others dissolved into giggles while I struggled to make sense of what she'd said. Couldn't make the party? Something better to do? But they were here, weren't they? And then it dawned on me.

They hadn't arrived late. Dad hadn't paid them in. They'd been here all along, watching, waiting. They were here to laugh at me. My cheeks flamed.

'Look!' Faye sniggered. 'Her face matches her hair!'

I wished a hole would appear in the ice, a hole I could fall into and disappear forever. It didn't of course. I was vaguely aware of Emily and Meg just behind me, and I knew that Mum, Dad and Cass were here somewhere too. I tried to turn, to get away from Chelsie's cold eyes and Faye's twisted smile, but the blades slipped beneath me and I fell down, hard, with the sound of laughter in my ears.

Emily crouched beside me on the ice. 'Ignore them,' she said kindly. 'Come on, Ginger. Don't let them win.'

By the time I crawled on to my hands and knees, Chelsie and the others were skating away, looking back at me over their shoulders. 'Honestly!' I heard Chelsie say. 'She looks just like a pig . . . a fat, ugly, ginger *pig*.'

When I think back, that's the bit I remember. The shame, the hurt, the ice freezing my grazed palms and numbing my heart. I'll never forget it.

Emily and Meg helped me to the edge of the rink, and I told Mum, Dad and Cass I'd hurt myself falling. We all clomped off the ice, handed in our boots and went up to the cafe for burger and chips – only I couldn't eat a single bite of mine. Mum brought out the chocolate layer cake and lit the candles, and everyone sang 'Happy Birthday'.

My eyes slid away from the cake and down towards the rink below, where I could see Chelsie and Jenna and Carly and Faye skating round and round: laughing, tossing their hair, flirting with boys. I hated them, sure, but a part of me wanted to be like them too.

I blew out the candles and made a wish.

They say you should be careful what you wish for, but, hey, I got what I wanted – I'm in Year Eight now, and things are very different.

You *can* make a wish come true, if you're determined. You can put the past behind you, be somebody new, and that's what I did. I moved on. These days, I try not to think about the sad, scared little girl I used to be . . . she's in the past, and that's a place I'm not going back to, not ever.

Could YOU be a STAR?

Have you got the sparkle to really shine? Find out with our fun quiz!

1) You're spending a whole Saturday with your friends. You:

a) Splash out and be waterbabes for the day, getting fit and checking out the cute lads at the local pool.

b) Hit the shops, trying on the poshest dresses you can find. After all, one day you'll be rich and famous . . .

c) Hang out at the skate park, listening to cool music on your iPod and hoping nobody offers you a go on their skateboard!

d) Plan a day full of fun, with something each of your mates will like – if they're happy, you're happy.

2) You're feeling low. How do you handle it?

a) Go for a long run or cycle ride to take your mind off it – exercise always cheers you up.

b) Pretend nothing's wrong. Act like you're happy, and pretty soon you will be!

c) Hole up in your room listening to loud, gloomy rock tracks – those bands really know how you're feeling.

d) Call your friends and talk things through – between you, you can fix almost anything and beat the blues.

3) You've been asked to sign up for an after-school activity. You choose:

a) Netball club . . . it's fun, fast and helps you stay fit, plus you love the competitive bits!

b) The school play. OK, so you're only painting scenery, but you're learning all the lines in case the lead actress drops out!

c) Orchestra. While everyone else is playing the clarinet, you're hammering out an MCR song on the school drum kit . . .

d) The anti-bullying scheme – you want to help other kids get their lives back on track.

4) Your pic's just been in the local paper. Why?

a) You won all your events at the latest karate contest, and were pictured with your trophy.

b) You persuaded a roving reporter to interview you – who cares what it was about, you might be talent-spotted by a Hollywood agent!

c) A photographer snapped you in town, thinking you were part of the Halloween celebrations, but it was just your everyday look . . .

d) You've just raised £100 for a local animal sanctuary by dying your hair pink!

5) Of all your achievements, you're most proud of . . .

a) the time you completed the local mini-marathon in record time.

b) the time you played an angel in the school nativity play!

c) the time you won the karaoke contest on holiday.

d) the time you rescued a kitten from drowning.

Add up your score and find out what kind of star YOU are!

Mostly **A**s:

You're a **SPORTS STAR** – fit, healthy and bursting with energy! You can be competitive, but you're a good team player too – whatever you set your mind to, you can achieve!

Mostly **B**s:

You're a **MOVIE STAR** – and any day now, you'll be ready for your red-carpet moment! You love drama, glamour and acting – and not just on the stage. Remember us when you're famous!

Mostly **C**s:

You're a **ROCK STAR** – cool, funky and not afraid to stand out from the crowd. OK, so today it's recorder lessons and singing in the shower, but tomorrow it'll be centre stage at Glastonbury . . .

Mostly **D**s:

You're a **SUPER STAR** – you're not looking for fame, fortune, gold medals or red carpets, but you could be the brightest star of all. You're kind, caring and thoughtful – a friend in a million. Go, girl!

cathy cassidy
tells all

Where do you get the ideas for your stories?

I get ideas from all around me – things I see, hear, read, remember, imagine . . . then I daydream, and sometimes the ideas turn into a story!

What's the best thing about writing stories?

I get to imagine being all kinds of different characters and dream up a million different situations, so life is never dull or boring! It's so cool watching a daydream unfurl on paper . . . and knowing that my readers get to share that daydream is brilliant too!

If you couldn't be a writer, what would you be?

I've been everything from a waitress and petrol-pump attendant to an art teacher and an agony aunt . . . but if I had to start over, I'd run an animal sanctuary or be a craft worker making weird textiley things.

What do you like to do when you aren't writing?

I'm addicted to reading – especially teen books! I also love swimming, eating cake with friends, music festivals, tepee nights and anything arty/crafty.

What advice can you give to aspiring writers?

1. Read lots – you'll learn all about plot, style and dialogue as you go.
2. Write – practise, practise, practise – then practise some more!
3. Write about what you care about – it'll show in your work.
4. Carry a notebook to jot down ideas/thoughts.
5. Daydream. It's free exercise for the imagination – all of my stories start off that way!

And now for the crucial quick fire-questions:

What's your favourite . . .

COLOUR? Moss green

WORD? Chocolate (sigh . . .)

ANIMAL? Llama (but donkeys and hares are cool too!)

PLACE IN THE WORLD? Either the Galloway hills or the west coast of Ireland, but Sri Lanka is awesome too . . .

NUMBER? Don't have one – I'm allergic to numbers!

BOOK? *The Catcher in the Rye* by JD Salinger, a fab American teen book from the 50s . . . but I have a million fave books, so it's hard to choose just one!

Follow your dreams with all cathy cassidy's gorgeous books

Catch all the latest news and gossip from

cathy cassidy
at

cathycassidy.com

Top gossip direct from Cathy

Sneaky peeks at new titles

Details of signings and events near you

Audio extracts and interviews with Cathy

Post your messages and pictures

Groovy downloads

Ideas for holding your own Friendship Festival

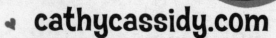

cathycassidy.com

Don't miss a word!

Do you want to find out all the news about

cathy cassidy

as it happens?

Sign up to receive a **free email newsletter** from Cathy every month! You will receive the latest gossip straight to your inbox every month, and you'll be the first to know about books, events and the exciting new stuff!

AND you will get an **extra special newsletter** from Cathy through the post every time a new book comes out.

Go to **cathycassidy.com** now to sign up

cathycassidy.com

Hiya . . .

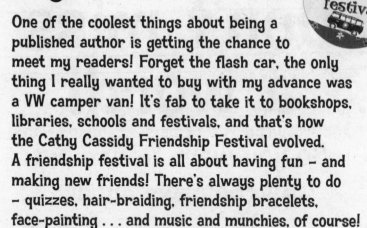

One of the coolest things about being a published author is getting the chance to meet my readers! Forget the flash car, the only thing I really wanted to buy with my advance was a VW camper van! It's fab to take it to bookshops, libraries, schools and festivals, and that's how the Cathy Cassidy Friendship Festival evolved. A friendship festival is all about having fun – and making new friends! There's always plenty to do – quizzes, hair-braiding, friendship bracelets, face-painting . . . and music and munchies, of course!

Friendship is something worth celebrating, so why not use these ideas to put on your own Friendship Festival . . . go for it!

Cathy Cassidy
x

Getting ready:

- Send all your friends an invitation telling them where and when the Friendship Festival is happening

- You could ask everyone to dress up for the event and maybe award a prize for the best outfit

cathycassidy.com

On the day:

- Set the scene by decorating the venue with brightly coloured streamers and balloons

- Announce the start of the Friendship Festival and explain how Cathy tours the country with her van

- Gather everyone together and read a chapter from one of Cathy's books

- Friendship bracelets are great fun to make. All you need to do is buy some brightly coloured thread and then plait three strings together. It's easier if you work in pairs and get a bit of adult help to start you off

- There are lots of other things you can do to make your Friendship Festival really special, such as hair-braiding, funky music, make-overs, hand-/face-painting, nail art, T-shirt customizing, drinks and munchies, competitions, sleepovers, henna tattoos and lots of other craft activities (e.g. making bookmarks out of thread and beads). Have fun!

cathycassidy.com

BEST FRIENDS are there for you in the good times and the bad. They can keep a secret and understand the healing power of chocolate.

BEST FRIENDS make you laugh and make you happy. They are there when things go wrong, and never expect any thanks.

BEST FRIENDS are forever,
BEST FRIENDS ROCK!

cathy cassidy's
My Best Friend
Rocks!
enter at
cathycassidy.com
mizz
award